Louisa Heaton lives on Hayling Island, Hampshire, with her husband, four children and a small zoo. She has worked in various roles in the health industry—most recently four years as a Community First Responder, answering 999 calls. When not writing Louisa enjoys other creative pursuits, including reading, quilting and patchwork—usually instead of the things she *ought* to be doing!

Also by Louisa Heaton

The Baby That Changed Her Life
His Perfect Bride?
A Father This Christmas?
One Life-Changing Night
Seven Nights with Her Ex
Christmas with the Single Dad
Reunited by Their Pregnancy Surprise
Their Double Baby Gift
Pregnant with His Royal Twins

Discover more at millsandboon.co.uk.

A CHILD TO HEAL THEM

LOUISA HEATON

MILLS & BOON

First published in Great Britain 2018
by Mills & Boon, an imprint of HarperCollins*Publishers*
1 London Bridge Street, London, SE1 9GF

Large Print edition 2018

ISBN: 978-0-263-07298-3

This book is produced from independently certified FSC™ paper to ensure responsible forest management. For more information visit www.harpercollins.co.uk/green.

Printed and bound in Great Britain
by CPI Group (UK) Ltd, Croydon, CR0 4YY

For the real Tasha, Bonnie and Lucy.

CHAPTER ONE

SHE COULDN'T SEE the road. There were too many people criss-crossing in front of her. This way. That. Seemingly with no order to their lives.

Women were heading home from the market with goods balanced in baskets atop their heads, babies strapped to their backs in swathes of fabric. Cattle chewed the cud at the side of the road, as if bored with life, idling alongside market traders who were much more vibrant, calling out, selling their goods—brightly patterned fabrics, spices and vegetables—whilst loud pop music blared from speakers she couldn't see.

Her nose was filled with the scents of food—fresh fish, caught that day, being the strongest.

Tasha Kincaid urged her off-roader forward, sounding the horn as much as she could. Thick, choking dust was being kicked up from the tyres as she revved the engine, desperate to get through the crowds, anxious to get back to the *Serendipity*, on the far side of town, because of her passenger, lying on the back seat, unmoving.

Children were not meant to be this still. This quiet.

The *Serendipity* had anchored just two days ago. She'd taken the children in her class to see it. The vast vessel, a floating hospital ship, sat there in the waters of the Mozambique Channel, waiting to give aid to those who needed it for free.

The children in her class had drawn pictures of the boat, and she'd used the lesson to teach them about kindness and giving. About helping others. They'd even been able to go on board briefly and talk to one or two of the nurses, who had generously given their time.

Maria and Rob were from Ireland and were volunteers, helping out on board for six months before returning to their paying jobs back home.

Back in class, she had pinned the children's pictures to the peeling walls of the classroom, instantly brightening up the place with their happy colours. That had been the day she'd first found herself worrying about Abeje.

Abeje was Tasha's star pupil. She tried not to have favourites. All the orphaned children in her class were special, brilliant and curious. But Abeje was different.

She had been orphaned at a young age after both her parents had died, and the only home she'd ever known was the Sunshine Children's Centre. She'd never had a proper family, but she was bright and intelligent. A deep thinker. A philosopher. And she wanted to be a doctor.

The similarities between them had struck Tasha hard. She recognised that gleam in her eyes. That yearning and thirst for knowledge. To do well. She wanted to let Abeje know that she could be anything she chose to be—that Tasha would help give her that chance. That the whole world could be hers as long as she pursued a passion.

But on the day they'd visited the *Serendipity*—the day that Tasha would have expected Abeje to be at her most attentive, her most intrigued and excited—Abeje had seemed somehow *off*.

A little listless. A little tired, and complaining of a headache.

All children got sick. It was inevitable. So when Abeje hadn't come to school the next day Tasha had figured she was probably just taking a day to recuperate. Knowing that Abeje had no mother or father to soothe her brow, she'd thought it might be a nice gesture to go to the children's centre and check on her, take her some pretty flowers to brighten her room. Just to let her know that she was being thought of and worried about.

But the second she'd seen Abeje, semi-conscious and sweating, Tasha had known that there was something to be worried about. With the matron's blessing, she'd scooped Abeje up into her car and had screeched away in a trail of thick red dust in an effort to get to the hospital ship.

The vehicle hit a pothole and Abeje moaned as the car bounced them around in their seats. Tasha risked a quick glance. The poor girl was drenched through with sweat and the sun was glaring down at them, burning everything it cast its gaze upon.

'Not far now, sweetie! We're nearly there...just stay with me!'

Horrible thoughts were rushing through her head—meningitis, encephalitis. Maybe a water-borne infection? A slideshow of horrific images passed through her brain, courtesy of the books she'd once studied.

She could smell the docks as they inched closer. The heat, the brine, the dust. The fish caught during that morning's outing were only now being brought back to port. Fruit, meat, chickens in cages were all piled high, the chickens squawking and flapping, the busy trade causing human traffic that she had to struggle to get through.

She cursed quietly, biting her lip, hitting the horn in frustration as the giant sides of the ship loomed over her—so near and yet so far. The car was surrounded by a thick crowd of people and she was making minimum progress.

Growling, she stopped the car, put her keys in her pocket, scooped Abeje into her arms and began to push her way through the throngs of people.

'Excuse me! Sorry! Can I just squeeze through?'

Suddenly she was at the gangplank, Abeje heavy in her arms.

She ran up it, panting in the heat, sweat prickling her underarms, her back. The coolness of the ship's interior was welcoming. The air-conditioning a blessing. For her, at least.

Desperately she tried to remember her way around the ship from the brief tour they'd taken a few days ago. The emergency clinic was down this corridor.

Hefting Abeje into a firmer grip, she ran down it and burst through the double doors into the clinic, where there was a twenty-bed ward. 'I need help!' she yelled at Maria and Rob, who were making up a bed with new sheets.

Tasha ran to a spare bed and laid Abeje down upon it as gently as she could. The two nurses moved towards the bed.

'She's sick! I don't know what's wrong, but I think it's serious! Please help her!'

She stepped back as the two nurses rushed forward. It was hard to fight the urge to do something herself. To let go. To give her precious charge up into a stranger's hands.

'What's going on?'

The male voice instantly cut through the haste. Authoritative. English. The sort of voice that made you turn around and pay attention to the speaker.

It was a voice she'd heard before. One that took her right back to her childhood.

To that moment.

Him.

It can't be...

Surely she was wrong? Memories were fickle, and she'd done her level best to forget his very existence. How he looked. How he *sounded*. The voice that she had once closed her eyes to listen to.

Tasha glanced over her shoulder...

At the man that had once torn her heart in two.

Only now her heart was galloping, her head was pounding with incredulity and her mouth was dry, clogged with all the dust from the road. She was aware of sweat drenching her skin.

How can it be him?

How is he here? In this place?

They'd been children. She just thirteen years old. Him three years older. And it might have been an adolescent crush, something silly, but she remembered the pain and the humiliation all too well, even now. It was like being that teenage girl all over again.

'*Quinn?*'

The doctor frowned at her briefly, clearly wondering how she knew his name, but then his attention was returned to Abeje, who lay still on the bed. 'Tell me her symptoms. When it began.'

Tasha blinked hard, still not quite believing that he was *here.* Of all the places in the world he might have gone he was *here.* On *this* ship.

As if from a world away, unable to tear her gaze from his face, she began to relay Abeje's symptoms, stunned into numbness and a creeping sense of hurt. The box she'd put him in, and all her feelings about him—the box that she'd locked and hidden away for all these years—was finally beginning to crack open, creating a canyon of a scar upon her heart.

There was something about the tall blonde who had just appeared in his clinic. Something weirdly familiar. But he didn't have time to place her. He'd thought he knew most of the English people here in Ntembe, but obviously not.

Perhaps she was new? She had corkscrew honeyed curls, deep blue eyes and a mask of sun-kissed freckles across her nose. Cute.

But he didn't have time to think about her, much as he would like to. She wasn't the important one. The most important female at this point in time was the semi-conscious one lying on the bed—not the one who somehow knew his name.

Quinn examined the young girl, his stethoscope already in his ears, the metal diaphragm at its end already upon her clammy chest. She was about six years old, a little underweight, but not so much that it concerned him. She had a temperature of nearly one hundred and three degrees, sweats and chills. Drowsy. Flu-like symptoms.

His first concern was malaria. 'Has she been vomiting?'

The blonde shook her head, curls shimmering. She looked terrified. Almost as if she were afraid to look at the little girl on the bed. As if she was shutting herself down.

'I don't know.'

'Any family history I should know about?'

She shook her head, looking at him in apology, cheeks colouring.

'I don't know.'

'Has she been given anything?'

There was a pained expression in those blue eyes of hers.

'I don't know. I'm sorry. I'm just her teacher.'

He listened to her heart. It sounded good, if a little rapid. Her chest was clear at the moment. Checking her eyes and the palms of her hands, he saw she seemed pale, and the possibility of anaemia assured him that malaria was probably the case here.

'Let's get her on an intravenous drip and get some blood drawn so we can do a rapid diagnostic test. She's probably going to need anti-malarials.'

'You think this is malaria?' the woman asked, heartbreak in her voice.

'It looks like it. The bloods will let us know for sure. You're her teacher?'

She looked frightened. On edge. Her arms were wrapped around herself protectively, making her look smaller.

'Yes.'

'Are any of your other students sick?'

She shook her head. 'I didn't think… I'm sorry. I don't know.'

It seemed there was a lot she didn't know. But he didn't want to get frustrated with her. This wasn't the first time a patient had turned up at the ship with no one knowing anything about them. Sometimes they'd get dumped there. Abandoned.

'Can I sit with her?'

'You've taken anti-malaria tablets before coming over here?'

She nodded.

'Good. Then you can stay.'

There was something about those eyes of hers. Something familiar. Oceanic blue and just as deep. Thick, dark lashes enveloping them. Where had he seen them before?

He held out his hand, determined to find out. 'Dr Quinn Shapiro.'

Hesitantly she took his hand, as if she'd been asked to touch a live, hissing and spitting cobra. 'Tasha Kincaid.'

Tasha Kincaid. The name didn't ring a bell. Perhaps he was mistaken about her being familiar somehow? Some people just had that type of face…

Though she seems to know me...

'Nice to meet you.'

She looked at him strangely. Questioningly. Surprised. *Relieved?*

'Likewise.'

Nice to meet him? Quinn Shapiro? Here on the *Serendipity*? Of all the hospital ships in all the world, he had to be on *this one?* Off the coast of Africa? What were the chances?

She didn't want to think about what he'd done. What he'd said. About how he'd made her feel. *So small. So unimportant. So ugly.* Those feelings she'd stamped down on long ago, determined not to let them affect her self-confidence.

It had been a struggle for a while, especially because she'd been at such a vulnerable, impressionable age, but she'd done it. The only way she'd been able to carry on had been to pretend it had never happened.

Tasha sat by Abeje's bed, holding her student's hand. Abeje was sleeping now, her face restful in repose, her chapped lips slightly parted. Her skin was hot to the touch—boiling. Her small body was fighting a battle that had no definite outcome. The rapid test, which had given a result within minutes of their arrival, had shown that it *was* malaria.

'Don't you die on me,' she whispered to her small charge, hoping that her just saying those words would make some higher power hear them and infuse the little girl with a fighting spirit.

'Do you hear me? You've got to pull through this. You've got to fight it. You can't give in.'

'How's she doing?'

Quinn's voice behind her had Tasha leaping to her feet, her heart thundering like galloping horses, her cheeks flushing red. She turned around, stared at him, resisting the urge to start yelling at him. To humiliate him. To embarrass him the way he had once done her.

Trying her best to hold the bitterness back, she said, 'She's sleeping.'

'That's good. Her body needs rest.'

Yes, it did. So did she. But her own tiredness, her own endless, exhausting fear, was something she had to dismiss right now. Her body was once again thrumming to the presence of Quinn Shapiro, apparently having forgotten that years ago she'd made a decision never to be attracted to him ever again.

Who knew the human body could be so treacherous? It apparently had a mind of its own...was reacting to him in ways she couldn't control.

He clearly didn't recognise her. The last time

she'd seen him she'd been thirteen years old, chubby and grubby, and he'd been sixteen. Just three years older, but seemingly so worldly-wise, so mature, so stunning. And so handsome. With a dazzling smile that had made her heart go pitter-pat.

Her newly teenaged little heart hadn't stood a chance when Quinn had first appeared on her radar. Tall and rangy, with a blond quiff, captain of his school's rugby team, he'd had an easy charm and boy band good-looks. She, on the other hand, had found comfort in food and books, and her wild mass of unconquered curls had earned her the nickname Nit-Nat. Just because she'd once caught nits and spread them to the other kids in the children's home.

She'd never thought that was fair. It could have happened to any of them. Every time she'd itched and scratched, her fingers buried in the mass of her thick curls, the other kids would run away from her, laughing. She'd spent many hours in front of the matron, painfully enduring the process of the nit comb that kept getting stuck in the knots of her hair. They'd even used a special shampoo, but it had stunk, earning her even more nicknames.

Her misery had been punctuated with happiness at Quinn's visits. She had been regularly ensnared by Quinn's smiles and friendly open manner to the other kids at the home when he'd visited to pick up his best mate Dexter.

Her crush on Quinn had been absolute! She'd drawn hearts in her notebooks and put her initials and his inside them with a little arrow. Signed her name with his surname—*Natasha Shapiro.* It had looked so exotic, so stylish, so grown-up. Everything she had not been, but aspired to be.

She'd try to chat with Dexter, as casually as she could, trying to get information. Quinn wanted to travel the world. To be a doctor. To change people's lives.

Could he have been any dreamier?

His dreams she had decided to make hers. She'd always enjoyed medical dramas on the television. Always liked to try and guess what was wrong with people and sometimes would get it right. So she had decided that she, too, would go to medical school when she was older. She would travel the world and treat people and make them better and everyone she tended to would be just so grateful to her. Thankful to her for saving their lives. She would be adored. Loved at last. No one would look down on her ever again…

But it hadn't worked out that way. Following someone else's dreams had only brought her nightmares.

'I wonder if you could do me a favour?' Quinn asked.

Once upon a time she would have jumped to do any favour he'd asked of her. But now she felt cautious. Wary of getting hurt again. Wary of awakening that mean streak he'd once unleashed upon her.

'What is it?'

'I need you to check on the other children in your class and at the children's home. Could you do that for me? Report back if any of them are sick?'

She thought about his request. Was it possible

that the others might be sick? She hadn't even considered the idea. Once she'd seen the state Abeje was in her only thought had been to get *her* help.

'You think they might be?'

'It's a possibility. The bloods show we're dealing with the parasite plasmodium falciparum. It's an aggressive strain. We're treating with chloroquine and ACTs.'

Tasha frowned. 'Because some falciparum parasites are immune to the chloroquine?'

He raised a single eyebrow. 'That's right. How did you know?'

She shrugged. 'Oh, I…er… I think I read that somewhere. Before I came over here.'

'Well, it's just as a back-up.'

She thought about having to leave the ship. Leave Abeje behind. 'I don't want to leave her alone.'

'She's in safe hands.'

Of course. Of *course* he would say that. *He* still believed in medicine and his skill to save this little girl's life. Her own belief was a little more battered. But then, as his words began to have more potency the longer they lingered in her brain, she thought about the other children in her class—Machupa, Tabia, Claudette, Habib and the others—all those little faces, all those little people she had come to care so much about. She knew she had to do the right thing and go and check on them.

'Of course. You're right. I'll go right now.'

She had to get away from him. Needed some breathing room. Some time to think.

'Wait.' He held up his hand as she moved to slink past him. 'I think maybe I ought to come with you—and you need to have a drink first. It's the middle of the day and you've had nothing since your arrival. You need to hydrate.'

Her stomach was churning. How would she be able to drink anything? He wanted to go *with her.*

'I can do it by myself,' she said quietly.

What's happening to me? How has he turned me into a mouse again?

'I insist. Abeje doesn't need her teacher collapsing on her as well, does she?'

Tasha sat down in her chair and looked at the sleeping girl. So young and already fighting for her life. How much more bad luck did she need to experience at such a young age? There was no one else to sit by her bedside. Just Tasha. And, yes, she *did* need to look after herself. No one else would do it for her. But she felt herself bristling at his suggestion. Ordering her about. Telling her what was best for her. Even more so because he was right.

I'm going to have to deal with it.

If the other kids were sick, wouldn't it be better to have a *real* doctor by her side?

'Okay.'

'How do you like it?'

She blinked. 'What?'

'Your tea.'

He smiled, and the devastating power of it—the familiarity, the punch-in-the-gut strength of it—almost winded her. Those teeth… That dimple in his right cheek…

Remember what he did to you.

'Er…milk. One sugar.'

His eyes creased as he smiled again, bookending the corners with lines that had never been there before, but that just increased his attraction. How did the nurses get any work done around him? How did anyone concentrate? Were they immune? Had they had some sort of vaccination? Because if they had then she damn well wanted one for herself!

She'd worked *so hard* to forget this man. And she'd thought she'd been successful. It had just been a crush, as a child—so what? He'd broken her heart badly—but who cared? It had been years ago. *Years.*

And it turned out he didn't even recognise her.

Or remember her.

If she was so forgettable, then she wanted to make sure he meant just as little to her now.

She did not need his help or advice. She knew what she was looking out for. And the idea of spending more time with him when she wasn't prepared for this unexpected onslaught only made her feel sick.

He was not the man she wanted by her side.

* * *

Quinn hauled himself into the passenger seat as Tasha gunned the engine. There seemed to be fewer people about now, the morning market trade dissipating, so she was able to reverse easily and begin the drive back to the Sunshine Children's Centre.

Her nerves were on edge. She felt prickly. Uncomfortable. He still hadn't recognised her and she was in two minds about telling him who she was.

If Abeje recovered quickly, perhaps there would be no need to tell him anything? But her gut reaction was that Abeje was in for a long fight and that it would take some time before they saw any signs of recovery. Malaria was an aggressive disease in this part of the world still, and she'd racked her brains to try and remember what she knew about the condition.

A single mosquito bite was all it took to get infected, and most people showed symptoms within a couple of weeks of being bitten. The terrible thing was that it could be fatal if treatment was delayed. She could only hope that they had got to Abeje in time. A combination of drugs was slowly being dripped into Abeje's system through an IV. She hoped it was enough.

'What made you come to Africa to teach?'

So he wanted to do small talk? Though she wasn't sure if *any* talk with him would ever be small for her.

'I just did.'

The desire to keep her life away from his scrutiny was strong. He'd already ridiculed her once. It might have been years ago, but that didn't mean the pain was any less. Being with him now made her feel raw again. Unguarded. The wound in her heart, open to infection.

'You've always taught English?'

'No.'

'What did you do before?'

She glared at him as she drove, before turning back to keep an eye on the road. It was none of his business.

'This and that.'

'Mystery woman, huh?'

Without looking at him, she knew he was smiling. She heard it in his voice. He really had no idea, did he?

So two-faced! Trying to charm a woman you once thought so little of.

'What made *you* take a post on the ship?'

There was a pause before he answered, allowing time for the potholes in the road to bounce them around, so that their shoulders bashed into each other briefly before the car was righted again.

'I needed a change. I'd spent some time working in British hospitals, but I felt like stretching my wings. I didn't want to become stale, you know? Complacent. I needed a new challenge.'

'Well, Africa certainly does that to you.'

He nodded. 'It does.' He turned to look at her. 'Did you come out here for a challenge?'

What could she tell him? That she'd come here on pure instinct? That teaching at schools in the UK had worn down her spirit?

Such long, gruelling hours, weighed down by the gazillions of reports and lesson plans and resources she'd had to create. Hours spent on assessments and figure-juggling that would never see the light of day but had to be there in case the inspectors turned up. Weeks spent worrying about work politics and staffroom gossip and pressure from the senior management team to be constantly at the top of her game.

She'd just wanted to teach. She'd wanted to forget all the rest and get back to what she enjoyed. Seeing the face of a child light up with understanding. Being with children who were *eager* to learn. She'd wanted to get back to grass roots. Find her joy again. Her spirit.

Africa had always seemed to her an exotic place—both beautiful and dangerous at the same time—and after going to a seminar in which the speaker had talked about her time teaching in Senegal she'd found an agency and signed right up. She'd needed to get away from the everyday. She'd needed to find something special.

And she had. It had brightened her heart, coming here. Given her exactly what she'd needed.

'I came out here to make a difference.'

He nodded in understanding. 'I know what you mean.'

She doubted it. She imagined that Quinn's life had always been rosy. Nothing too horrendous or upsetting for *him*. Surely he must have cruised through life? Privileged and well off?

Tasha drove on through the hot, dusty streets of Ntembe. She was glad that Quinn had made her drink that tea. She *had* needed it. And now she was hungry, too, but that would have to wait. They had children to check up on.

She parked the vehicle outside the centre.

The Sunshine Children's Centre was a long, low building, with a corrugated tin roof and a hand-painted sign made by the children. There was a bright yellow sun in one corner, its rays stretching across the sign, behind the words, and in another corner, if you looked hard enough, beyond the accumulation of dust, there was a child's face with a big, happy smile.

'This is it.'

'How many children live here?'

'Fifty-three. Most of them girls.'

They got out of the car and dusted themselves down. 'How many of them are your students?'

'Ten—though others go to the same school. They're just in different classes.'

'We should check them all—hand out anti-malarials just in case.'

She nodded. Yes, it was best to err on the side of caution. Preventative medicine was better than reactive medicine.

'Okay. I'll introduce you to the house matron—her name's Jamila.'

'Lead the way.'

She led him into the interior, explained the situation to Jamila and told her what they wanted to do to check on the children. Permission was given for them to treat them.

Tasha was glad it wasn't a school day, so the children were all at the centre, though some of the boys were out at the back, playing football. All seemed to be in good health. None of them were showing signs of illness or fever.

'Looks like Abeje was the unlucky one.'

Jamila stepped forward. 'Abeje travelled with an aunt back to her village two weeks ago.'

'With Ada?' Tasha asked.

'Yes. The village is about a two-hour drive from here. Do you think she could have got infected there?'

Tasha looked at Quinn and he nodded. It was a distinct possibility.

'I wonder if anyone is sick at the village? Is it remote? Do they have any medical facilities nearby?'

Jamila shook her head. 'The *Serendipity* is the closest they have.'

Quinn frowned. 'They might feel they're too sick to travel. Perhaps we ought to go out there? Check on everyone?'

'Do you have enough medication?'

'We'll have to go back and restock. Maybe get a nurse to come along, too. You'll come, Tasha, won't you?'

At one stage in her life she would have jumped at the opportunity. But this was different. She didn't need to go if Quinn and a nurse were going. As far as they knew she was just a teacher. They didn't need her. Besides, she wanted to stay here and keep an eye on Abeje. Taking a trip with Quinn was her idea of hell!

'You won't need me.'

'Nonsense! As Abeje's teacher you'll be able to explain why we have to do this. Introduce us to the aunt. Talk to the villagers.'

'I barely know Ada. I've met her maybe once. Perhaps twice.'

'More times than any of us.'

The way he was looking at her was dangerous. As if he *needed* her. *Wanted* her. Desperately. And it was doing strange things to her insides. Confusing things.

Okay, so more hands on deck might help get the medication distributed more quickly, and she couldn't expect him to take many medical personnel from the ship to help. Some of them needed to stay behind. To look after Abeje, for one thing.

She could feel her resolve weakening and she

hated that. Just like before, she was being pulled deeper and deeper into Quinn's world.

'Fine. Okay.' She nodded quickly, hating herself for giving in. Imagining already how difficult it would be to spend so much time in his company.

'Great.' He beamed. 'And whilst we're getting there you can tell me how you know me—because I sure as hell can't place where you're from.'

She froze as he walked back outside.

So there *was* something, then. He recognised her as being familiar, but couldn't *place* her.

How would he react when he realised she was *Nit-Nat?* How would he feel? Would he have forgotten what he did? What he'd said? Who she was? How he'd destroyed her little heart in a matter of minutes?

She wanted him to suffer. To feel uncomfortable. To apologise and grovel for her forgiveness…

Part of her wondered if it was better just to pretend she didn't know what he was talking about. To insist that they'd never met before. But a stronger part of her wanted to let him know their connection. Their history. To surprise him and have him see how she had changed. She was no longer a chubby, nit-infested, braces-wearing girl in secondhand clothes.

She had not changed for *him*. She'd just grown up and been battered by life in so many ways. Life had given her plenty of challenges—killing her parents when she was young, making her grow up in a children's home, having Quinn humiliate her, her job destroy her and her marriage break down. And yet she had come through it all. Was still standing. Still able to find joy in her life. To enjoy it. To feel worthwhile.

Was fate, or karma, or whatever it was called, finished messing with her life?

She hoped so. But the fact that she was here and Quinn was here and they were together made her suspect that fate hadn't finished putting her through the wringer just yet.

Tasha stepped out into the sunshine, shielding her eyes from the worst of the sun's rays. She climbed into the vehicle, started the engine and turned to look at him, butterflies somersaulting in her stomach, her mouth dry.

It was time. She had to say it.

Just say it. Get it out there.

'You do know me. I'm Tasha Kincaid now—but you might know me by my former name, Natasha Drummond.'

She saw him frown, think, and then his eyebrows rose in surprise as his eyes widened.

'That's right. You're in a car with Nit-Nat.'

CHAPTER TWO

NIT-NAT? SHE WAS NIT-NAT?

When she'd first said her name his mind had gone blank. Natasha Drummond? Nit-Nat? He hadn't recognised those names at all. And then a small tickle of a memory had suggested itself. A sense of something appalling. Something he couldn't quite grasp, slippery and evasive. Something about that name being familiar. Something about that name being unpleasant.

Then he'd realised. It was something shameful. A memory he had tried to suppress… And then the memory had become stronger, fiercer, until it was roaring loudly, like a lion, right up in his face, and the hot breath of fetid shame was washing over him as he remembered what he'd once done.

He'd been fifteen years old the first time he'd

become aware of her. Although perhaps 'aware' was the wrong word. She'd just been one of the many background faces at the children's home where his best friend Dex had lived.

He'd always been fascinated by them each time he went to the children's home, simply because of what they represented. He was one parent away from being there himself, having been raised by his ex-Marine father because his mother had walked out on them. The children at the home had been a bright example of what his life might have been like if his father had left, too.

He'd gone there for Dex, so that they could play footie, or rugby, or cricket. Or simply just go for a wander, try to hook up with girls. He'd never paid much attention to the other kids at the home, but there had been one stand-out girl there. But she'd stood out for the wrong reasons.

Overweight, always a bit sweaty-looking, she'd had a thick mass of hair that had never looked combed. Metal braces on her teeth.

And the worst thing…? She'd had a crush on him.

Dex had told him.

'Nit-Nat's got the hots for you, mate! You're in trouble!'

'Why do you call her Nit-Nat?'

'She's got bloody nits! They're all caught up in that mop she calls her hair! They can't escape! I reckon it's one massive nest!'

He'd wrinkled his nose in disgust. Nits? They were always sending letters from school to parents telling them to be vigilant against nits. He'd remembered having them himself once, when he was about seven or eight—not that he'd been about to tell Dex that.

Dex had had great fun teasing him about Nit-Nat fancying him. It had been a running joke that never seemed to go away. Quinn had hated it. He'd worked so hard to perfect his image amongst his friends. He'd wanted to be known for going with the hottest girls of his year—not for the disgusting crush Nit-Nat had on him!

He'd tried to laugh it off, tried to ignore it, and he'd even once got angry with Dex for going on about it. In the end he'd let it wash over him, pretending to play along, pretending to be mortified so that the joke wasn't on *him* but on poor, misguided Nit-Nat.

The crush had become more and more obvious each time he'd visited Dex—almost to the point that he hadn't wanted to go there any more and had asked Dex to meet him somewhere else. That had worked for a while. He'd stayed away for a good six months. And then, when even *he* had forgotten about it, he'd made the mistake of calling in on Dex at the children's home.

She hadn't changed. In fact she'd seemed thrilled to see him.

'Quinn! You're back!'

She'd beamed a smile, revealing all that metal.

He'd been appalled. *It wasn't over.*

'Hi.'

'You here for Dexter?'

'Yep.'

He hadn't wanted to give her anything. It had been embarrassing, the way she'd stood there—thirteen years old, her hair a frizzy mess and her round body forced into a dress that was at least one size too small. Those buttons had looked as if they were about to burst apart.

'Haven't seen you for a while.'

'I've been busy.'

'What with?'

'This and that.'

'Did you know there's going to be a party this Friday?'

'Nope.'

'It's for Lexi. She's sixteen. We all get to bring a friend.'

'That's nice.'

'Would you come as my friend?'

He'd stared at her in horror, and realised her invitation had been timed perfectly to coincide with Dex's arrival down the stairs.

Quinn had looked at his friend, hoping he hadn't heard, but it had been plain by the look of awesome amusement on Dex's face that he had heard *every word.*

He'd been embarrassed, not at all happy that she'd had shamed him this way again when he'd been trying to be so cool and standoffish. He'd had to make it stop. Had to make that crush of hers end. And the only way he'd known how to do that at the time was to be brutally blunt.

Only it had somehow tipped over into cruelty.

He'd grimaced, walked right up to her.

'You realise you're ugly, right? And fat? And that there are so many things living in your hair they could do a nature documentary over five seasons?'

He'd looked her up and down, unaware that loads of the other kids in the home had gathered round to see what all the shouting was about.

'If you were the last girl on earth I'd probably kill myself!'

He'd seen the look of horror on her face. The way her cheeks had flushed bright red. The way tears had welled up in her eyes and had begun to run roughly down her ruddy cheeks. And he'd hated what he'd said, but hadn't been able to stop himself.

'The only boyfriend you could ever get would be a blind one.'

And then he'd grabbed the gaping, gawking, laughing Dex.

'Let's go.'

Dex had ripped into him for hours after that, and he'd spent days feeling angry and ashamed that he'd treated someone like that, made her feel small just so he could maintain his street cred with a friend.

He'd not been brought up to be that way. His dad had raised him to be respectful of women, despite the way his own wife had treated him. He'd been taught never to bring another person down, but instead to make yourself better. Despite his mother walking out on them, he had *never* heard his father badmouth his wife.

And what had he done? Believed his reputation to be more important. Believed that being 'one of the boys' was more important.

He'd never gone back to the children's home after that. He'd not wanted to see the hurt in Nit-Nat's eyes. Not wanted to be reminded of what he'd done. And the only way he'd been able to cope had been to push it to the back of his mind, pretend it had never happened and bury the shame beneath mountains of other stuff. Fighting the urge to go and apologise the way he knew he should.

He hadn't thought about her *for years*. Why would he? He'd been just sixteen when it had happened. She had been thirteen. It was ancient history. So much had happened since then. Other stuff had taken precedence, as was wont to happen in life.

Until now.

He'd never believed they would ever be face to face again. The world was a big place to get lost in.

Quinn sucked in a breath, his heart pounding in his chest, the shame from all those years ago flooding him like a tsunami of regret. He knew what he ought to say. Right now.

I'm sorry I hurt you. I apologise. I never meant to do it. I hated myself for it.

'Tasha, I—'

'You know, I *know* we were just kids, but I was thirteen years old. *Thirteen!* You were my first love. The first boy I lost my heart to. Now I know why they call it a crush. Because when you're rejected and humiliated in front of everyone it *feels* like you're being crushed. That's what you did. That's how you made me feel. Tiny. Inconsequential. Stamped on from a great height. You could have just said *No, thanks.* I would have understood.'

He watched as she gunned the engine, put her hand on the gearstick to shove it into first gear.

Quinn laid his hand upon hers. He didn't want her to start driving yet. He had to tell her. Had to let her know.

'I'm so sorry. I behaved appallingly. I know I did. You won't believe me, but I was incredibly ashamed of what I said to you. It haunted me. I wasn't raised to act like that and yet I did, out of some misguided belief that my credibility with my friend was more important than your heart. I felt guilty for ages.'

She yanked her hand out from under his. 'Good. I'm glad.'

'I really am sorry, Tasha. I should never have hurt you.'

'Well, you did.'

She stared at him for a moment, those eyes of hers welling up once again. As the first tear dripped onto her cheek she revved the engine.

'Let's get back to the ship.'

And then she was driving.

He sat in the passenger seat beside her and gazed at her profile as she concentrated on the road. The curls had been tamed and glinted golden in the hot African sun. She had a soft caramel tan and her blue eyes were steely and determined. The set of her jaw showed she meant business and wouldn't take any crap from anyone.

He knew he had to make it up to her. Make up for all the years of hurt and anger she must have carried inside because of him.

Tasha Kincaid—once Natasha Drummond—had certainly grown up. The puppy fat of youth had disappeared with the braces and she'd emerged as a beautiful young woman. A gazelle—long-limbed and graceful. He'd seen the possibility in her back then. But kids were kids and anyone different—fat, bespectacled, red-haired—was an object for their attempts at humour.

He vowed that he would show her the way a woman *deserved* to be treated. That he would be charming, caring and kind. He would build her up and replace her harsh memories of him with something more wonderful.

He hoped he could do that.

He'd originally asked her to go with him to introduce them to Ada and the villagers because he'd wanted to spend more time with this enigmatic woman who knew his name and somehow seemed familiar.

He didn't regret asking her. Because now he knew it was important that she came with them. Because he needed more time with her.

Time to put things right.

Before Quinn's humiliation of her they'd once gone on a trip together. Years ago—when they were children and Tasha's home had organised a visit to the zoo. Everyone had gone along, and somehow Dexter had wangled a place for Quinn on the bus.

The boys had sat at the back, loud and vocal, but Tasha had been at the front, very aware that Quinn was there.

She'd worn her best dress—a pale blue number, with tiny daisies on it—white ankle socks and scuffed patent leather shoes. Hours had been spent in front of the mirror, trying to tame her hair, but the more she'd combed it the frizzier the curls had become, so in the end she'd tied it back with a red bow, wanting to look her best for Quinn. She'd practised her smile in front of the mirror before they left, trying to work out the best way to do it so her braces didn't show too much.

She'd said hi to him when he'd arrived in the morning, barely getting a nod of acknowledgement in return, but that hadn't mattered. She'd offered him a drink and fetched him a glass of juice from the kitchen. He'd taken it, smiled at her and said, *'Thanks, Nit-Nat.'*

Her little teenage heart had almost exploded with excitement. This dashing, handsome, blond-haired young stud had smiled at her! Said her name!

And then he'd said, *'You look nice today.'*

It was the only thing he'd got to say to her before they'd left but she'd dined out on that compliment for days. It had warmed her. Had made her feel good. All gooey inside and yet shy. He'd liked her dress. Liked what she'd done to her hair. She vowed to do her hair like that all the time if he liked it that way.

She'd wanted to turn and smile at him on the bus but she hadn't, knowing that Dexter would wind her up about it, so she'd spent the trip staring out of the window, intently listening to everything she could—hoping that he might be talking about her in a nice way.

He never had been.

Her day had been spent half looking at the giraffes and the wolves and the lions and monkeys, and half sneaking glances at Quinn and having little hopeful dreams about their future together.

She'd wished she had a camera, so she could take his picture and put it in her bedroom.

He'd wanted to be a doctor and so had she. She'd imagined them working together at the same hospital. They would save lives! He would look at her after a long day together and thank her, and give her a hug, and then they would go home together, because of course they would be married. And at home it would be even more blissful than at work. She would have beautiful little blonde-haired children, with big blue eyes, and they would take them with them on their many trips around the globe.

None of that had ever happened, of course.

But here they were today. Together again. In Africa. Hopefully off to save some lives.

Maybe all she'd ever needed to do was wait?

It didn't take him long to inform the personnel on the ship of what they were doing. The staff seemed excited about the idea of a road trip, and as they busied themselves in preparation for a possible mass vaccination Tasha found a moment to check on Abeje.

She was asleep. Sweat beaded her brow and pooled in the dip at the base of her throat. Her breathing was rapid.

Tasha laid a hand against the little girl's skin and winced at the heat. *Poor thing.* She let out a breath and took a moment to centre herself. She could remember being poorly as a young child herself, with no one to sit by her bed, to soothe her brow or just to give her cuddles and good-night kisses. It had been so lonely.

Quinn knew who she was now. It was an even playing field. And, though she'd been worried about telling him who she was, now that it was out in the open she felt glad. He had a lot of making up to do if he was ever going to be in her good books again. He'd apologised, but that was too little, too late.

You should never have hurt me in the first place.

He deserved to spend some time wriggling on the end of her hook. She knew she ought to be gracious and allow him to show her who he was *now*. They *had* both been children. But…

He'd always said he was going to be a doctor. Always said he was going to travel the world. And here he was, doing just that. She liked it that he had stuck to his grand plan and was doing something worthwhile and noble. It showed her he wasn't still that cruel teenage boy he had once been. That there was more to him now.

It would have been so easy for him to have stayed working in a hospital in the UK, with modern equipment and civilisation and technology all around him, but no. He had come out here. To treat the needy, to give aid to those who had none.

That was a good thing to do, wasn't it? Heroic?

So you get some Brownie points, Quinn. I get that you're not all bad.

Tasha reached for Abeje's hand as a nurse, Rowan, came up to her.

'She's doing okay. I know it looks like nothing is happening, but we have to wait for the medications to work.'

Her Irish accent was lilting and musical. Even reassuring in a homely way.

'How long should that take?'

'It depends how long she'd been sick for, before we got the meds on board. The parasite she has in her system is quite an aggressive one.'

'It could kill her.' It wasn't a question. Tasha knew the risks of this parasite.

'We need to hope for the best.'

Rowan was not saying yes or no. Not promising that everything would be all right.

Tasha knew how to do that. She'd done it herself. But she'd never realised just how frustrating it sounded when she was on the receiving end of it. When you were worried sick about someone you needed someone in charge to tell you it would be okay. That they wouldn't die. This vagueness, the non-promise, was devastating, but as a doctor she'd always assumed her vague answer would be comforting. Would give hope.

'Will you keep an eye on her whilst I'm gone?' she asked Rowan.

'Of course. There won't be any change for a

while, so it's probably best that you're out there doing something else. It'll help keep your mind off it.'

Tasha wasn't sure that was true. She was hardly going to forget Abeje. The little girl was almost like a daughter. Not that she'd ever had one. But she definitely wanted children some day, and this was how she imagined it to be—worrying constantly. Fearing for their wellbeing.

'You'll contact me on the radio if there's any change?'

'Of course I will. It's a good thing you're doing. Going to help those villagers.'

Tasha nodded and Rowan walked away. It felt strange to her that she was going out with a medical team. It had been such a long time since she'd walked in their shoes, and it felt a little terrifying to be returning to it.

The last time she'd made a field trip with a hospital team had been out to the London bombings, back in 2005. There had been carnage. Injured people lying in the streets. Blood. Screams. She shuddered just remembering it.

What would they find in Mosa? A whole village wiped out? One or two people ill? Everyone healthy?

She hoped for the latter. Steepling her hands, she closed her eyes and began to pray to whatever god might be listening.

The *Serendipity* had a truck. Quinn and Tasha sat up front and two of the ship's nurses sat in the back, along with all the medical equipment and drugs they might need. It was a two-hour drive to the village from Ntembe, and if they got out there by mid-afternoon they could have everyone vaccinated by late evening—in time to drive home again. If people were sick they'd brought tents to stay in overnight.

Quinn was driving, his muscular forearms wrestling with the wheel as it reacted to the rough road surface.

'So, tell me something good.'

Tasha looked across at him. Something *good*? Sure. She could do that. In fact she yearned to make him see that she was happy and successful.

That what he'd done had not had any profound effect on her life. That it had not left her scrambling for any scraps of self-esteem she might have had left. Yes, he'd torn her down, but she had rebuilt herself and done so in spite of him.

'Qualifying as a teacher was a good day.'

He smiled, nodding. 'That's great! Which uni did you go to?'

'I did my PGCE at Kingston.'

'Fantastic! You must have felt very proud when you passed.'

She had. But not as proud as she had been when she'd qualified as a doctor. That had been after many years of hard work—not just one. But he didn't know that teaching had been her second choice. Her fall-back position.

'It was a lot of hard work. Lots of essays.'

'Universities *do* like those essays and dissertations.' He smiled again. 'Tell me what it felt like the first time you had to stand in front of a class of kids.'

She sighed, thinking back to her first placement. The one that had almost made her quit.

The out-of-control kids, their jeering and taunts. It had reminded her of how she'd felt once before.

'The first one was awful. They send you out on two-week placements during training. It was like putting a kitten in front of a pack of baying, rabid dogs. The students were awful. Teenage boys. Laughing and disrespectful. On my first day I ended up running from the room in tears.'

She didn't add that she'd felt particularly raw to teasing from teenage boys. Surely he must understand that? That she'd been weakened by him from the get-go and had never stood a chance? How it had made her feel like she was Nit-Nat all over again.

'I'm sorry.'

'It wasn't your fault, was it?'

But maybe it was? Maybe he'd made her ripe for the picking? Those boys had sensed her nerves. Her weakness. One of her first lecturers had talked about *showing no fear*. Said that some kids were like packs of hyenas, looking to wear a newbie teacher down.

'No, but…'

'My second placement was much better. Great kids—attentive. Determined to do well. The contrast in the two places really surprised me, but it was a lesson for me to persevere. I could so easily have given up after that first experience, but I think, in a way, that you toughened me up. I was determined to carry on and succeed. Lippy teenage boys weren't going to ruin my life.'

He nodded. Smiled. 'Lippy teenage boys are mostly cowards. Perhaps the only way they knew to deal with someone better than them, was to try and tear them down.'

She smiled back. 'Well, they failed.'

'I'm very glad to hear it.' He was solemn.

'What was it like the first time you had to treat a patient?'

He laughed, clearly relieved that the conversation had taken a brighter turn. 'Awful! I took the patient's history okay, but then I had to take a blood sample. Something I'd done in practice many times, that I thought I was good at, but I couldn't find a vein. The guy was like a voodoo doll by the time I'd finished with him.'

She smiled, imagining it. Remembering the first time *she'd* taken blood from a real, live patient. She'd actually done okay, even though her hands had been shaking with nerves. And her patient, a wonderful old lady, had been so kind to her. *'Everyone has to learn, ducky,'* she'd said.

'Ever lost someone?'

The question just came out, and the second it did—the second she realised what she'd said out loud—her cheeks flamed hot. Why had she said that? Why had she asked? Of *course* he was going to say yes. *Every* doctor had had someone die on them.

'Too many,' he answered politically. Non-specific. No details. Answering but not telling her anything. 'It's hard. You tell yourself you're ready. Your lecturers and mentors try to prepare you. But…'

Tasha stared at the road ahead, terracotta sand and rocks, scrubby bushes and thorny trees. A chorus of insects could be heard faintly above the roar of the engine.

'You can never be ready for loss.'

She looked at him. At the rigid set of his bristled jaw. His knuckles tight upon the steering wheel. He'd been the one who had first introduced her to loss. To pain and grief. She'd thought she'd known what that was, not having parents. But he'd provided her with insight into another kind with his hurtful words.

Perhaps he was right? Perhaps he *had* been a coward? Afraid to let his friend Dex see him as someone else.

'No,' she answered. 'You can't.'

The village of Mosa hoved into view just after four in the afternoon. It wasn't big—twenty or thirty homes at the most. Large brown cattle grazed by the side of the dirt road and the villagers working in the fields stopped their work to stare at the truck as they drove past. They probably didn't get a lot of visitors.

Quinn parked the truck and they all got out gladly, pleased to stretch their legs and work the kinks from their muscles. It hadn't been a long drive, but it had been a hot one, with the air-conditioning in the truck temperamental.

Tasha smiled at one of the villagers. 'Hello. My name is Tasha, and this is Dr Shapiro and his two nurses. We're looking for Ada Balewa.'

The villager stared at her for a moment, and then silently pointed to a hut further down.

She beamed a smile. 'Thank you.'

Together they walked down the track, towards the primitive hut that had been indicated.

'Ada Balewa?' she called out.

A small woman emerged from the depths of the hut, wrapped in a brown dress, frowning. 'Yes? Ah! Miss Tasha!'

Tasha smiled and greeted Ada with a hug. 'You're looking well.'

The other woman frowned again. 'Yes, I am, but I do not think that is why you are here.'

This was the part that Tasha had been dreading.

'Abeje is poorly. She was bitten by a mosquito and now she's sick with malaria. We have her in a hospital ship, but we thought maybe there might be some other people sick here. Can you tell us if anyone has a fever?'

Ada nodded. 'Yes. A boy and a girl.'

'Could we see them? We've brought medicine.'

'I will take you to them.'

They followed Ada—Tasha, Quinn and the two nurses, Maria and Rob. As they walked Ada asked about Abeje. Tasha told her what she could. That everything was being done for her.

'I wish I could see her.'

'If there's room we could take you back with us.'

'I have my own children here. Crops to tend. I cannot leave.'

'Then try not to worry. We'll do our best for her.'

'Thank you.'

The boy and girl that Ada had spoken of were brother and sister. The boy twelve, the younger girl nine. They were sweating and had been sick.

Quinn was quickly by their side. 'Let's do the rapid tests—double-check this is what we think it is. In the meantime let's get them on IVs so they don't dehydrate.'

Tasha stood back and watched him work. He was a true professional. She'd seen it before with Abeje and now she saw it again as he cared for these two siblings side by side. They were conscious, so he spoke to them, keeping his words simple in case their English wasn't good. He smiled. Explained what he was doing. Told them not to be afraid.

Even if they didn't understand his words they would at least understand his kind, caring tone. His unthreatening behaviour. His empathy and desire to help. It was good for her to see it. This side of him. It gave her hope.

She wished she could do more. Instead she silently watched as he worked, anticipating and expecting his every move. His care of the two siblings was exactly what she would have done herself. It was hard to stand back and do nothing.

The rapid tests confirmed malaria so he started the anti-malarials. When he'd done, he turned back to Ada. 'Is anyone else sick?'

'No.'

'I really don't want to leave these children here. They need urgent care. Would you allow me to take them back to the ship?'

Ada nodded. 'I will speak to their parents.'

She disappeared from the hut.

Tasha stood in the doorway, afraid to stay, afraid to leave. 'Is it wise to move them right now?'

He frowned. 'We won't do it straight away. I'd like them to get fluids on board first. We might have to stay here the night. Give them time to rest…get them stable before we move them.'

She'd known it might be a possibility when she came, but she'd hoped they'd be lucky enough to escape with a quick visit. Now she would have to spend the night out here with Quinn.

Tasha gave him a nervous smile. 'I'll go and tell Rob. Maybe get started on setting up those tents?'

She went to find the nurse. Rob was standing by the truck with Maria. It looked as if they were counting the medicines.

'There's more than enough here to inoculate the entire village.'

Tasha smiled. 'Anything I can do to help?'

'It's probably best if we gather everyone in the same spot to explain what we want to do. Then we can set up a line and treat everyone.'

She nodded. It did seem the best idea. 'I told Quinn we'd get the tents set up for an overnight stay, too.'

'Good idea. Perhaps we all ought to get something to eat, as well,' Maria added.

The tents went up easily—even though Tasha had never put one up in her life. Rob was clear on the instructions and they worked well together as a team. Tasha cracked open some bottles of water, so they could hydrate underneath the hot African sun. Even though it was evening, and everything was a little cooler, they still poured with sweat.

She looked out over the horizon at the vast emptiness, the grey, stony mountains in the distance. It was so different here from in Ntembe. At the port city there was always a sea breeze blowing in—there always seemed to be air and noise and life. Here in Mosa it seemed more solitary, more empty. Quieter. She missed the busyness of people. The safety of numbers.

As she hugged her arms to herself Quinn came to stand alongside.

'You all right?'

'I've only ever known Ntembe. I thought I knew more. Thought I knew Africa. But I don't.'

'It's a place that can always surprise you. Its capacity to inspire, to fear, to amaze, will always keep you on your toes.'

She looked at him. 'How are the children doing?'

'As well as can be expected. I think they were infected earlier than Abeje. They're sicker.'

Fear welled in her gut. 'Are they going to die?'

'Not if I can help it.'

He stared at her, determination in every feature.

The inoculation line was long, but each and every villager had turned up to receive medication. Tasha could see that Quinn was very happy about that. Neither of them would have liked to leave anyone out, and Ada had been instrumental in speaking to the villagers *en masse* and getting their understanding and trust, translating to those who didn't understand English very well.

They sat around a small campfire later in the evening, drinking coffee with Maria and Rob, who soon disappeared for an early night, leaving Tasha and Quinn alone.

'They're a couple,' Quinn explained after the two nurses had left to share a tent.

That left one other tent. One *small* tent. For Quinn and Tasha to share.

She hadn't realised the two nurses were together. When she'd seen two tents in the back of the truck and then erected them she'd figured that the two men would share one and she and Maria the other. But obviously that wasn't going to be happening, and she felt apprehensive about being in such a small space with him.

'Oh. You knew we would have to share?'

'Yes. But I can sleep in the truck if that's a

problem. I promise you I can be perfectly trusted to keep my hands to myself.'

He poked at the fire with a stick, creating sparks, unaware of the physical ones he was sparking within her.

The idea of Quinn Shapiro letting his hands roam over her body made her feel infinitely hotter than the African sun could ever do. Right now she needed less of a fire and more like a bucket of ice water. She was imagining him looking intently into her eyes as they both lay on the ground, facing each other…

Oh, dear Lord...

She took a sip of scalding coffee and winced.

Beyond the light of the fire the nocturnal noises of the bush had begun—insects, hyenas, and she even thought she heard the roar of an elephant from somewhere. Miles away, but instantly recognisable.

She was surrounded by primal beasts. There could be tigers out there, lions, predators of all shapes and sizes. But she was only afraid of the man opposite her.

Okay, maybe not afraid of him. But afraid of how he's making me feel.

Her teenage self would have screamed with glee at the idea of spending a night with Quinn Shapiro in a tiny tent. But her adult self was more cautious. So many years had passed since she'd last known him and she knew that *she'd* filled in the intervening years with a lot of baggage. Had he? Apart from his childhood, she hardly knew anything about him. He could still be a jerk, for all she knew. Just because he *said* he wasn't, it was hardly a guarantee.

'So, what did you get up to after we lost touch?' she asked, determined to maintain eye contact, to see if he got shifty, or lied, or tried to evade her question.

But he looked straight back at her. 'School, college, medical training—all the usual suspects.'

'Ever get married?' Her pulse was thrumming like jungle drums in her ears, sweat beading her upper lip.

We've got to share a tent.

He blinked, the twinkle in his eyes fading as a shadow passed over his soul. 'I did. You?'

So...there is *something you're not telling me...*

'I did too.'

She thought back to the day she'd stood in that small register office and made her vows to Simon. They'd been so happy. Or at least *she* had, believing their vows would tie them together for ever. But the only vow Simon had truly honoured was his Hippocratic Oath.

'Well, I think we both tried to skip past that answer as quickly as we could, didn't we?' He grimaced, poking at the fire once again.

'Do you want to talk about it?'

'Do you?'

No, she did not. She did *not* want to tell Quinn about how her marriage had failed and destroy the image she was trying to create for herself. Successful, happy, teacher Natasha. That was what she wanted him to see and believe.

She'd always told herself that if she ever did run into Quinn Shapiro again she would make him see her as wonderful, glamorous and successful. Happy and content. She did not want to go down the road that had led to her marriage going down the pan.

'I think I'll get some rest. It's been a long, eventful day,' she said.

He smiled, not challenging her answer. 'It has. Get some sleep. Goodnight, Tasha.'

'Goodnight, Quinn.'

And she headed for the tent, hoping and praying she'd be fast asleep before he turned in.

Quinn hadn't got much sleep. He'd got up in the night a couple of times to check on the two children and change their IVs for fresh ones. Each time he had sneaked back into the tent and just lain there, thinking about his wife, Hannah.

He tried not to, as a rule. Thinking about Hannah made him feel unstable. Rage and grief would bubble up, making him feel angry and vengeful. He didn't like the feeling that thinking of her could make him lose control at any minute. He didn't like the chaos inside him when he thought about Hannah.

So he did what he'd been taught to do by his father—pushed it all inside. Stamped it down.

'Boys don't cry!' his father had said. *'You stay strong—like a man.'*

Being strong. Gritting his teeth, thinking of other things, had worked. In fact his job had helped him the most. There were always sick people needing help. There were always lives he *could* save, even if he hadn't been able to save hers.

Theirs.

He swallowed and looked away from Tasha, not allowing himself to think of his wife and child. How odd that he had come all this way and found Nit-Nat. It had all started with this girl. The rules he had set down for his life had all begun with her.

Don't hurt anyone.

Always heal.

Always save life.

Saving the many could save you.

And Tasha lay beside him, unaware of just how much she had affected him back then.

She probably believed that he had been nonchalant about what he'd said. That he'd just walked off with Dex and forgotten about it, or bragged about it. *Laughed* about it. But he hadn't. He'd brooded on it for days, weeks, months.

He'd hated the terrible feelings he'd had inside—feelings that he'd caused through his own callous, unthinking behaviour. He'd wished he could apologise, but when he'd finally got up the strength to go back there, to face her and tell her he was sorry for what he'd said that day, Dex had told him that she'd been fostered out.

She'd never come back after that. His chance had been gone. And so he'd sat outside that home on a brick wall, underneath the window that had been hers, and he had vowed, out loud, that he would never hurt a living soul ever again. He had hoped, somehow, that she would *feel* the sense of his vow. That his earnest feelings would somehow carry across the world, through time and space to wherever she was, and somehow make her feel better.

Now she was by his side. Asleep, her face in repose, those curls spread out on the red ground sheet, her pale freckles masking her nose and eyes, her nose upturned at the end in a gentle slope, her lips full and parted…

The urge to kiss her came out of the blue.

He sat up abruptly, startled by the feeling. He crawled from the tent and stood outside, stretching, sucking in the morning air, and decided the best thing for him and Tasha was to have a little space between them. If he'd kissed her she would have been startled, for one, but would she also have thought that he was somehow pitying her, or something? Making up for those years lost in a childhood crush?

Whatever. It's crazy whichever way I think about it.

But as he marched across the campsite, towards the hut that contained the two ill children, his mind wrestled with images of her face in serene sleep. How much it meant to him to have her by his side. To have a chance to put right the things that had haunted him.

And to know just what it might feel like to take her in his arms…

CHAPTER THREE

TASHA WAS IMPRESSED with the speed at which Quinn worked. Watching him was fascinating. Almost hypnotic.

They'd set up two small cots on the flatbed of the truck, rearranging their equipment and medicines so that there was room for the two children, their parents and the two nurses. Then they stood and said goodbye to those that had gathered.

'We've done what we can, Ada. We'll try and get this family back to Mosa as quickly as possible.'

'Thank you so much. Please hug Abeje for me. She is very precious. My sister's only child.'

'Of course.' Tasha gave the woman a hug and then they all got back into the truck so they could head back to the ship. They leaned out of the windows and waved as Quinn turned the truck in the opposite direction and began to drive.

He seemed different this morning. More work-focused, if that were possible. When she'd woken he'd been gone, and she'd fought with feelings of relief and disappointment.

There'd been some anxiety in her about what waking up with Quinn might be like. Would it be awkward? Would he tell her that she snored and talked in her sleep, as Simon had always complained? But then opening her eyes and finding him gone had been sad, too. Part of her had wanted to wake up and see his face on the pillow next to hers. She'd wanted the chance to lie there and study his face, to look at the man Quinn had become. So many years had passed…

The road was as bumpy as she remembered, and for the first few miles she said nothing, just stared ahead through the windscreen, occasionally looking out and spotting gazelles, or scavenger birds whirling in the sky, soaring on the morning thermals. But the silence in the truck was wearing her down. Yesterday he'd asked her lots of questions. Today he was like a monk who had taken a vow of silence. What had changed?

'Did you…er…sleep okay?'

He shrugged. 'A bit. I got up a few times to check on the children. Changed their IVs. I got a few hours.'

'I can drive if you want the chance to get some more shut-eye.'

'Thanks, but I'm okay. It's only two hours to Ntembe.'

'And when we get back you'll have a long workday. You'll be exhausted.'

'Awake enough to look after my patients—don't worry.' He smiled. 'Doctors have survived on less sleep than this.'

Survived, yes. Thought clearly? No.

'And that's when accidents happen.'

She didn't want to think about her own mistake. The sequence of events that had led to her quitting medicine. It was exactly this kind of ill-advised bravado that Quinn was gushing that caused tragedies in the first place. She should know. And they were returning to the boat, where he would have to look after not only Abeje but the two children currently in the back of this truck.

'Stop the truck and let me drive.'

'Honestly, I'm fine.'

'Quinn! Stop the damned truck!'

He frowned, turning to look at her. 'Are you okay?'

'I'll be better knowing that you've had some decent rest before we get back to that ship.'

'If you're worried about my ability to look after Abeje, I can reassure you—'

'Reassurances mean nothing, Quinn. They're just words. Would you *please* put my mind at rest and allow me to drive?'

He thought about it for a moment. Checked his watch. Looked at the road ahead. Then he gave her one last look. 'You're sure?'

'I'm *very* sure.'

Quinn pulled the truck to a stop, the brakes screeching in protest.

Tasha had taken over the driving, but he felt a little confused by how angry she'd got. He sat in the passenger seat, frowning, wondering if she thought he would be a danger to Abeje.

'What was that all about?'

'Nothing. I was just being safety conscious, that's all.'

'So that was just you being a teacher and doing…what…a risk assessment for the trip?'

'Not just the trip, no. I want you on good form and well rested when you get back to the *Serendipity.*'

'You don't think I'll look after Abeje well enough?'

She let out a sigh. 'I'm sure you will, but doctors work long hours and push themselves when they really ought to take a break, and exhaustion can have an effect on their decision-making skills. If anyone's health suddenly took a turn for the worst I'd want your brain firing on all cylinders and not just one or two because you think you're Super Doc.'

'I can assure you I never think of myself as that.'

He turned away and closed his eyes, welcoming the opportunity to get the rest she was offering him. It *had* been a long night and he had lied. He hadn't got one or two hours' sleep at all. He'd barely got forty winks. He'd been up and down, checking on his patients, and in between staring at Tasha as she slept, trying to work out how she made him feel. How much he needed to do to repair their past.

'Good. So do me a favour and shut up and sleep.'

He smiled sleepily, feeling exhaustion slowly claim him. The warmth of the day, the rocking of the vehicle, the hum of the engine…all served to lull him into unconsciousness.

He didn't wake until the screech of the brakes woke him again, and they were portside to the *Serendipity.*

No one could have been more happy to see the *Serendipity* than Tasha was. She wanted to see Abeje, and she wanted to know the two children in the truck would be in a hospital, where they ought to be. She was also exhausted herself. It had been a long two days. She was tired, hungry and thirsty. And she was covered in dirt from the road. She needed a shower. She must look a sight.

Next to her, Quinn yawned and stretched.

'Wake up, sleepyhead. We're back.'

He smiled, rolling his shoulders, working out the kinks. 'You got us back here in one piece, then?'

'I *can* drive a truck. Does that surprise you?'

'No. I'm sure you have all kinds of skills I know nothing about.'

Tasha looked down at her hands.

You'd be surprised.

'I'd like to come on board and see Abeje before I head off to work. Is that okay?'

'Sure. We've got staff showers you can use if you want to freshen up.'

She ran her hands through her hair and her curls released a spray of red dust around her in a halo. 'I think that's probably a good idea. I must look a sight.'

'You look absolutely fine.'

Fine? *Fine?* That was almost as bad as *You look nice.* Damning with faint praise. But what else was he going to say to her? That she looked gorgeous? Beautiful? Stunning?

'Thanks.'

But she flinched backwards as he leant in towards her, his hand reaching out. *What is he doing?* She could feel herself begin to panic. Her breathing increased, her heart pounded, her mouth went painfully dry.

His fingertip swiped a line of red dust from the slope of her nose.

He wiped the dust on his shirt and grinned at her, opening the truck door to get out. 'You've got half the road on you.'

And then he disappeared out of her sight to go to the back of the truck.

Tasha sat there for a moment, steadying her breathing, wondering just what the hell was going on in her insides. He just had to look at her, smile at her, touch the tip of her nose and her body went into overdrive!

What was *that* all about? Was her body still remembering the crush she'd had on him? Or was this something new? Something infinitely more powerful? More primal?

Perhaps it was something she ought to be afraid of…

Tasha's shower made her feel more human. She stood under the cool spray and let the water run off her body, revelling in the refreshing flow until she suddenly remembered she had a class to teach today and there was no time for standing around.

She towel-dried her hair, wincing at the wildness of her curls, and then headed off to check on Abeje.

There'd been no change. Not for the better, anyway. Abeje was sleeping, so Tasha went to check on the other two children.

'How are they doing?' she asked Quinn, patting down her hair, hoping it wasn't going crazy and wild in the heat.

'They're stable.'

Stable. Another one of those medical terms that was so politically correct. Neither giving hope nor taking it away. So no one could be blamed.

'Have you done the bloods?'

'Yes. We've just sent them off to the path lab.'

'They're on the chloroquine and ACTs?'

He nodded, looking at her strangely.

She folded her arms, a surge of frustration flooding her body at not being able to do anything to help except watch and wait as Quinn took the children's observations, marking them on a chart.

Temperature. Blood pressure. Heart-rate. Respirations. Oxygen saturations.

Numbers. Always numbers deciding someone's chances. Numbers and statistics had ruled her life at the children's home, too—the chances of being adopted as a teenager, the likelihood of girls being preferred to boys, the fact that the longer you stayed in a home, the less chance you'd have of being adopted.

The day she'd turned thirteen her hopes of being adopted had plummeted. No one would take her. No one had wanted her in all these years—why would they take on an unruly teenager? Each day had added to the fact, depressing her, and only her crush on Quinn had brightened her day.

Looking at him now, just on the other side of the bed from her, reminded her of what it had been like to watch him as a young girl. He'd always seemed so out of reach. So unattainable.

'I'd better get back. I've got a full day of teaching.'

'Well, you're welcome to come and check on your young charge whenever you've got a spare moment.'

'I'll come round straight after I finish—later today.'

'Great. Maybe we could have a coffee or something?'

She flushed. She couldn't help it. Years ago she would have bitten his hand off in excitement. Now she was more wary, worried about what it might mean.

'A coffee?'

'No strings. Just two old friends spending time together after a long day.'

'I don't know…'

'Come on, Tash. We've both changed. We're both different now. We've moved on. Let's not dwell on the past.'

'The past is what's made me who I am today.'

He smiled. 'And I'd love to know more about who you *are* today. Give me the chance.'

That smile… That smile of his was powerful. Did he realise what it did to her insides? She could still see that sixteen-year-old boy in that smile, but there was also the man too—and boy, oh, boy, that man had a come-to-bed smile.

She was scared. Her entire body felt his pull, but the logical part of her mind was desperately trying to remind her of how cruel he had once been. How much he had hurt her.

But didn't he deserve a chance to show her that he was different?

She nodded quickly, before she could change her mind. 'Okay. Coffee.'

He smiled. 'Great. I'll see you later.'

As she walked away all she could think of was *him.* The time they'd spent together so far. The way their pasts bound them. All that had gone before…all that was still unwritten.

Her feelings for him were strong, but what *were* they, exactly? Friendship? Attraction?

It was hard to ignore the fact that she still felt attracted to Quinn. Because she'd rather hoped that all these years of thinking of him as the bad guy would have wiped out the teenage crush that had begun all those many moons ago.

Was this a bad idea? Was agreeing to coffee the wrong thing to do? Their relationship was from the past—perhaps it was best to leave it there? Undisturbed.

I think it's too late.

She was already involved. She was already *disturbed.* She couldn't help it.

She was drawn to him, wanting to know more about him, about what he'd done in all these years. If he'd ever thought about her, the things he'd accomplished, his dreams for the future. And she realised, as she sat at home with a cup of tea, that she wanted to share the details of her life with him, too. She wanted to talk to him about stuff. Things she'd done, things she'd seen, places she'd gone to.

He was her only connection to childhood. Her strongest memory.

He felt like home.

Abeje was awake when Tasha returned to the ship in the evening, and even managed to give her a small smile.

'Oh, you're awake! Hi, you. How are you feeling? You really had me worried.' She bent over and gave her a small kiss on the cheek.

'I'm tired, Miss Tasha.'

Tasha stroked the hair back from her face. Abeje's skin still felt hot to the touch, but not as bad as it had yesterday.

'Of course you are, sweetpea. But you've been getting some good medicine. You know where you are?'

'The ship.'

'That's right.'

She felt so much relief that Abeje was awake and talking. That her eyes looked clear and bright and that the anti-malarials Quinn had given her seemed to be working. She knew they weren't out of the woods yet, but maybe they'd got to Abeje early and stopped the parasites in their tracks?

'We did some creative writing today in class. Everyone wrote stories. They were really wonderful. You'd have liked that.'

Abeje smiled and then closed her eyes. When she was sure she'd gone to sleep Tasha got up from her bedside and pulled the curtain around her to give the little girl some peace and quiet.

The ward was quite busy. They had the three children in this ward, and next door they'd had some new patients come in, to whom Quinn had been called.

She figured if they were going to get a coffee it was certainly going to be a late one. Perhaps it would be best if she just left him to it? They could grab a coffee another day.

Reluctantly, she headed off the boat, and was thinking about going home and grabbing something to eat when she heard her name being called.

Quinn was waving to her from the deck. 'You bailing on me, Tasha Kincaid?'

She face lit up without her realising it. 'Not at all! I just thought you were busy.'

'I'm done! Hold fire and I'll be down in a minute.' He disappeared from view and she stood there like a young girl again, feeling all silly and excited, waiting for a boy.

The boy. Quinn Shapiro.

What am I doing?

She tried to remind herself that she was a grown woman, with a lot of water under the bridge. She tucked a stray curl behind her ears and sat on a wooden crate beside the dock as she waited.

Soon enough Quinn joined her, wearing a fresh blue linen shirt and khaki trousers. 'Hi. Ready to grab a coffee?'

'Actually, I'm starving. Could we get something to eat, too?'

'I wouldn't say no to that.' He smiled and took her arm, guiding her towards a small dusty and rusty car.

'This is yours?'

'Well, we're not stealing it.' He grinned, holding the door for her to get in.

It looked old. Dilapidated. As if he'd picked it up from a scrapyard rather than a dealership. Foam was bursting out of the torn seats.

'Does it work?'

'Like a dream. The aesthetic helps to deter thieves.'

Hesitantly, she got in, reluctant to touch anything in case it came off in her hand.

He got in beside her and started the engine. It fired first time.

Tasha looked out of the window and smiled.

What am I doing? she thought again.

Quinn drove them through Ntembe, occasionally having to sound his horn to clear the way, sometimes sticking his arm out of the window to wave and say hello to people he knew. He seemed popular.

'How long have you been here?' she asked.

'Only a couple of days.'

'But the entire port seems to know you.'

'We've docked here many times.'

Which meant he'd left many times, too. 'How long are you here for?'

'A month.'

A month! So in a few weeks he'd be gone again?

She wasn't ready for the onslaught of disappointment that hit her like a freak wave.

People always leave me.

'Where will you go next?'

'Madagascar is our next port of call.'

'Oh.'

He looked at her. 'Will you miss me?'

She looked away from him, out of the window at the passing streets, still filled with people on their way home from long working days.

'I haven't been with you long enough to miss you.'

The atmosphere in the car had changed. She appreciated that he was trying to be bright and perky, friendly and amiable, but she wasn't sure if she could cope with that from him yet.

'Maybe we should just stick with coffee,' she said.

Quinn quickly pulled over.

She turned to look at him and ask why. 'What are you doing?'

'I want to know what's wrong.'

'Nothing's wrong.'

'So why do you want only coffee now?'

Exasperated, she undid her seat belt and got out of the car. He'd stopped by a small field of what looked like sweetcorn. Between her and the field was a small irrigation ditch that smelt quite dank and dirty. It made her think about mosquitoes and malaria and sick children. About Abeje lying in her hospital bed, weak and feeble, whilst she was out gallivanting with a man who, by rights, she really ought not to be talking to.

And then there were thoughts of another child. A child she hadn't been able to save. She hugged her arms around her body, haunted by the past.

She heard Quinn get out, too and then he was by her side. 'What's wrong? Come on, Nit-Nat, you can tell me,' he said in a soft voice.

Tasha shook her head, angry. 'Don't call me that.'

‘Tasha.’ He stood in front of her, forcing eye contact.

‘I don’t know. I don’t *know* what’s wrong! I’m on a rollercoaster with you, Quinn! There’s no straight and steady…it’s all ups and downs! We shouldn’t be here. We should be back with those children. Healing them.’

He considered her for a moment. ‘There’s nothing we can do at the moment but wait.’

‘It’s not enough. There must be more we can do! I hate feeling helpless. Useless. It feels horrible.’

‘Hey…’ He lifted her chin with his finger, wiped away the tear that had begun to trickle down her cheek. ‘It’s okay.’

She had to ignore the sensation of his soft thumb sweeping across her skin. ‘Is it? How do we know we’re doing enough?’

‘Because I *know* we are. You have to trust me.’

She stared back at him, confusion, hurt and anger blustering through her with the force of a storm. Buffeted by emotions she didn’t want to feel. 'That's what it all comes down to, isn't it? Whether I trust you.'

He stared back at her. 'Well, *do* you?'

'I don't know. I want to, but…'

'Well, that's a start. It wasn't a no.' He smiled. 'Give me a chance—that's all I ask. A chance to prove to you that you can trust me.'

She looked up into his face. Into the face that had haunted her dreams for years. A face that seemed open and kind. The face of the man she so wanted to believe in.

She'd really like to close the door upon her pain. It had hurt for too long. Here was a chance. A chance to change that hurt into something positive. If it went wrong, what would she have lost? Nothing. But if it went right…

'Okay. One chance.'

He smiled. Nodded. 'That's all I need.'

They found a little café that neither of them had been to before and went in. The Coffee Bean was small and intimate, but it offered hot food, and it was open till late, so they decided to chance it.

The tables were old Formica, their surfaces indented with scratches, but the flowers on each table were real, their scent competing with the aroma of the food. Somewhere amongst the din music played from a radio.

Quinn and Tasha sat by the open door, so they could feel the evening breeze.

'So...what *really* made you come to Africa, Quinn? What made you think, *Okay, I'm going to leave the UK and head out on a hospital ship*?'

He laughed, but it wasn't a happy, genuine one. She watched his face carefully, wondering what nerve she'd just hit and how he was going to answer. It would have to be the truth. She would know if it wasn't.

'I needed a change. A challenge.'

'You were an A&E doctor?' That hadn't been her specialty. She'd trained in paediatrics. Thinking that caring for kids would add some joy to her day.

Quinn nodded.

'I would have thought A&E was challenging enough.'

'It was. I just...' His voice drifted away and his fingers fidgeted with the condiment pots on the table. 'English schools not enough of a challenge for *you*?'

She nodded. 'They were...'

'But...?'

Tasha smiled. 'But we were talking about *you*. You asked me to give you a chance and I am. I need to know more about you. What makes you tick.'

'I was married, as I said before,' he replied, looking directly at her. 'And it didn't end well and I... I just needed to get away.'

'How long did it last?'

Quinn let out a sigh. 'Eighteen months.'

One and a half years? I wonder what happened?

'I'm sorry.'

She sensed there was more, but he obviously wasn't ready to tell her just yet. Maybe if he knew something about *her*...?

'I was married to Simon. He was a doctor,' she explained, leaving out the fact that she'd been one, too. 'We had a whirlwind relationship, which initially started with a whole lot of lust and secret assignations in linen cupboards. We got caught once, which was embarrassing, by a nurse who'd come to fetch some clean pillowcases.'

Quinn smiled at her.

'We both seemed to want the same things. It was exciting, and thrilling, and so when he asked me to marry him I said yes and we went to our nearest registry office and did the deed, with two witnesses off the street.'

'Wow.'

'Was I impulsive? Crazy? Probably. It all went downhill once we'd signed the marriage certificate. It changed things between us. Subtly at first, but then more noticeably.'

'In what ways?'

She sighed. 'The *fun* seemed to go. We were official. Man and wife. We weren't those horny young people any more, looking for a thrill. I think he began to see me differently. I know I did the same to him. We were married. I wanted to plan our future, I wanted us to be serious. But getting married had somehow poured water on our fire. And then I discovered he was having an affair.'

Quinn frowned. 'I'm sorry…'

'We'd drifted apart. He thought the fun in linen cupboards would continue and I wanted a serious relationship. To have a family of my own.'

He grimaced. 'How long did *your* marriage last?'

'A year.' She laughed, then, realising the irony. 'Aren't we a great pair?'

He nodded, just as the server brought them their food. They'd ordered *poulet yassa*—chicken marinated overnight in peanut oil, lemon juice, onion, vinegar and spices—which was served with couscous and roasted plantain. The aroma was mouth-wateringly good and they tucked in with gusto.

'What was your wife's name?' she asked, her fingers dripping with the marinade.

'Hannah.'

She smiled. 'Why do you think we both failed so badly at marriage?'

He shrugged. 'I don't think we *failed.* I'm sure we both fought as hard as we could to save our marriages.'

There was something he wasn't telling her. But she didn't feel she could push because she knew damn well there was lots *she* wasn't telling *him.* But they'd made a good start. They'd begun to open up to one another. What they had would take time. Trust didn't happen overnight. And though she needed to trust him, he also needed to feel he could trust *her.*

'You're right. I didn't want it to fail, but Simon was the one who gave up on us. He didn't even try.'

Quinn swallowed a mouthful of chicken and nodded thoughtfully. 'There's nothing you can do if the other partner just gives up.'

Tasha raised her mug of coffee and held it towards him to make a toast. 'To friends that don't give up.'

He raised his mug and smiled.

'To friends that don't give up.'

* * *

Quinn drove her home. He was so very pleased that he'd met up with Tasha again. What he'd done to her in the past had always been a stain on his memories—one that he hoped he was now beginning to rectify.

It had been a little difficult to start with, but since sharing a meal and some conversation at The Coffee Bean he really felt that his friendship with Tasha was heading in a great new direction.

All he had to do was keep her as a friend and not ruin it by wanting more.

He always expected other people to give their all. Ever since Hannah had died—since *they* had died—he'd wanted other people to give everything. Not to give up when things got hard or painful.

Hannah had tried to protect him. She hadn't told him how bad her pain was. Insisted they were making the right choice in holding off treatment. He would never have gone along with it if he'd known how much pain she was in each day.

But she'd been so determined to give their unborn son life.

Their deaths had almost destroyed him. His wife's doctors—people he'd once thought of as friends—had also known the truth, and he hadn't been able to be around them again. Hadn't been able to walk in the same corridors and wards he once had. His workplace as much as his home had become tainted by lies and deceit.

He'd felt angry. Had wanted to lash out at everyone. And afterwards Hannah's family had blamed him. Blamed him for not doing more to save her. Their own guilt had been eating them alive, and they'd turned that pain on him.

It had been the safest thing for all of them for him to get away. To start afresh. To go somewhere there would be no memory of his wife at all.

The vacancy on the hospital ship had arrived at the perfect time and he'd jumped at it, determined to secure the post and get away from everything that reminded him of his loss.

He was glad he'd met up with Tasha. He'd been

able to shine a light on one of the dark spots in his past. He could rectify that in a way he couldn't with his wife or child. He was making it better and it made him feel good.

But *she* made him feel good, too. Being with Tasha was like breathing again after being in a vacuum. She made him feel brighter. Lighter. Unburdened. Her smile could light up the room. He didn't know exactly what it was, just that being in her presence made him believe that life could possibly be good again. And he liked that feeling. He wanted more of it.

More of *her*.

Who'd have thought that the freckle-faced curly-haired girl he'd humiliated in his long-lost past, might just be his saviour?

Quinn was determined to spend as much time with Tasha Kincaid as he could.

He was hungry for the healing warmth of her friendship and trust after being out in the cold for so very long.

CHAPTER FOUR

ABEJE WAS SHOWING signs of jaundice. A nurse called Quinn during the night and he got up to inspect the little girl. She had the shakes and was complaining of muscle pain and tiredness. The lack of red blood cells was causing it, but she was still producing urine so her kidneys hadn't been affected yet. He prescribed treatment, including a transfusion to aid her platelet count, and then went to check on the other patients in the clinic.

The two children they'd brought back from Mosa were sleeping soundly and reacting well to their medications, despite having received them after Abeje. There was a woman with a serious case of mastitis, and they were doing their best to help her work out the blockage in her milk ducts so she could continue to feed her baby. There was a middle-aged farmer with a suspected stroke, but they hoped to discharge him soon, and a patient awaiting surgery on a large goitre in his neck.

A mish-mash of cases, but he liked the variety in his work. The only cases he didn't deal with were obstetric. Maternity and pregnancy was a big no-no for him. Thankfully there were other doctors on board who *did* specialise, so he was able to hand over to them, but he did his best to stay away if he could.

He didn't like it. He had made an oath to treat all people needing help. So if there weren't any of those other doctors around he did it, because he had to, but inwardly he hated every second. And that hate came from fear. Fear that he would fail another mother-to-be. Fear that he would lose two patients in one.

It was too close to home. Cancer he could deal with. But pregnant mothers…? All he saw was Hannah.

Hannah with her burgeoning belly, sitting up in bed, smiling at him, holding his hand, despite the pain she was going through. The sickness. She'd refused chemotherapy to give their baby a chance at life, but the pancreatic cancer had been aggressive and had spread rapidly throughout her body. And she'd died before the baby could be saved.

Their son had been just twenty-two weeks in gestation, and though they'd tried to deliver him when his wife's system had gone into mass organ failure he'd not been strong enough to live. The steroids they'd injected her with to strengthen his lungs hadn't been enough. He'd been tiny. Almost see-through. A fragile body no bigger than his hand.

His son had struggled to live for a matter of hours.

He'd watched his wife die slowly, whilst she'd tried to keep their son safe and give him a chance. And then he'd had to watch his son die.

They'd let him hold him at the end. He'd unbuttoned his shirt and slipped his son's baby bird body onto his chest, barely registering his weight, tenderly cradling him. His son's minutely thin fingers had held one of his, and tears had dripped from his eyes, down his cheeks and onto his son's failing body.

He'd never felt so helpless. So impotent as a doctor.

He'd felt his son's last ragged, struggling breaths and he'd raged against a world that could let this thing happen to such an innocent young life.

Quinn had sat in that hospital chair, gazing at his son's face, memorising the shape of his eyes, his tiny button nose, his small mouth invaded by a tube, his little body covered in fine downy hair, and told him over and over for hours how much he loved him, how much his mother had loved him. How precious he was. How brave. And that it was okay to stop fighting.

He could let go.

He could stop.

The last juddering breath had come with a sigh, and when his chest had moved no more he'd held him for a long time, until his tears had run dry. The nurses had taken pictures for him and he had those now, in his wallet, never far from him at all.

If he'd lived he would be a little boy by now—Abeje's age—learning through play, making friends, laughing and having fun.

But instead his son was just a memory. A powerful memory that drove Quinn on, that gave him the courage to get through life. Because if he could survive losing his wife and son he could survive anything.

What could life do to him now? It had brought him Tasha and she was a *good* thing. He knew that.

They'd have a month together. Four weeks in which they could consolidate their friendship. Twenty-eight days after which he knew he would have to sail away from her, knowing that each time he returned to Ntembe she would be here. A reassuring presence. A smiling face to welcome him.

In the privacy of his office he took out his wallet and looked at the photo he treasured most.

He was a father. A father without a child. A husband without a wife. He'd had the most precious people taken away from him already.

He wasn't going to lose Tasha's friendship.

Not now he'd been given this second chance.

But as he stared at the photo, as he was reminded of his loss and the pain he had gone through, he felt hesitation. Hesitation about getting close to someone again, even if it was just as friends. Would he and Tasha ever be *just friends*? She'd had such strong feelings for him once. Had loved him. And he didn't want to be responsible for hurting anyone ever again.

He'd taken an oath not to.

The classroom wasn't the same without Abeje. Tasha really missed her presence, her bright, smiling face, her eagerness to learn. Her empty seat was a painful reminder that whilst the rest of them were there, learning about adverbs and adjectives, Abeje was lying in a hospital bed, fighting for her life.

It was hard for Tasha to stand there and concentrate when all her instincts were telling her she needed to be back on the ship. When all she wanted to do was sit by Abeje's bedside and whisper words of encouragement.

Malaria was a killer. Nearly half a million children died from it each year, most of them in Africa. It was a horrific number and she wished she hadn't looked it up on the internet last night, when she'd been searching for details on the disease, but she'd not been able to help it.

She'd known when she chose to come here that it was a country rife with it, but she'd naively believed that she wouldn't have to face it. That she would stand in a schoolroom, by a blackboard, chalk in hand, and the most pressing thing on her mind would be whether the children understood the rules of grammar.

She couldn't make a difference as a doctor any more, so she wanted to make a difference as a teacher. She needed to change someone's life for the better. She *had* to! Because what was it all about, otherwise?

She told her class that it was time to go out and play, and when they'd all filed out and the classroom was quiet Tasha went over to Abeje's chair and sat down on it. Lifting the lid on her desk, she looked inside and saw Abeje's books, all neatly lined up. She picked up the top one and looked inside. She saw Abeje's progress, from hardly being able to write to almost being fluent. Her mastery of the English language was evident in her sentences and stories.

Abeje was clever and special, and Tasha didn't know what it was, but she *felt* something for the little girl. A need to do more for her. A need to give her a greater chance in life. But how?

She put the book down and closed the lid, smoothing her hands over the old wood. She would go to visit her tonight. Straight after work. And perhaps she would see Quinn, too…

Just thinking about him lightened the feeling of burden that was upon her shoulders and in her heart. Last night they'd had a lovely time together. Just talking, sharing stories, laughing, enjoying being in each other's company. It was the start of a beautiful friendship. She knew that. They got on well together. Despite the past. She was glad she had chosen to be brave and give him the chance he needed.

This afternoon all the children were going to write letters to Abeje. Letters that would form a book. Letters that might make their friend fight to get better and come back. That would let her know that everyone was worrying about her.

It was something she herself would have loved when she'd been sick as a child. She'd once contracted the flu and had been stuck in bed for almost two weeks. Apart from one 'Get Well' card, Tasha had barely seen the others at all.

She'd been so alone. Frightened. Desperate for love.

She didn't want anyone else to feel that way.

'Abeje?' Tasha sat by the little girl's bed, holding her hand. She'd been alarmed when she arrived, to see how yellow her eyes looked. Jaundice was caused by a build-up of bilirubin in the blood and tissues, which in turn was caused by the breakdown of red blood cells. It wasn't a good sign, and her research last night was fuelling the fires of her worry. It might lead to coma. Kidney failure.

Death.

That kind of thought made her blood run cold.

'*Abeje?* It's Miss Tasha.'

'She's sleeping. She was awake a fair bit during the night,' Quinn interjected from behind her.

She hadn't known he was there.

'Was she bad?'

He took her arm and walked her away from the bed. 'I was called about the jaundice and we began treatment, but she had chills and shakes for a while, which kept her awake until they settled in the early hours.'

Tasha looked back at her. She looked so small in the hospital bed. Too tiny to be fighting a major disease such as this one. 'Alone…?'

'I stayed with her. She was never alone.'

Oh. That was kind of him. She smiled her thanks.

'She's getting the best treatment. We just have to give it time to work.'

'I know.'

She knew all about time and how important that was. She needed to be patient, but she wasn't very good at that any more.

'I feel so helpless. I read last night that the treatment for the falciparum parasite should be different according to geographical location. Are you sure she's on the right medicine?'

'I'm sure.'

'She has complicated malaria, though. Jaundice, anaemia, impaired consciousness…'

'She's okay.'

'But she's *not* okay! What made you choose the chloroquine and ACTs? She's under eight—she could have had the quinine-based regimen or clindamycin.'

He frowned. 'Hey, don't *do* this. You'll drive yourself insane. I appreciate that you care, and you're worried, but you have to trust me as a doctor as well as a man.'

But her faith in medicine had been weakened.

'I can't just sit here. Watching her. Waiting for her to die.'

He blinked. Stared back at her. 'She's not there yet. You need to find hope. Like the rest of us.'

She sighed. 'How do you do that?'

'You dig deep inside. You find the strength. You think you've got it tough? Well, it's harder for the patients. And they need you to be there for them. To hold their hand and tell them it's okay.'

She heard something in his voice. A little hitch. He'd been through something. Lost someone close. She could tell.

'How do you know so much?' She appreciated that he was a doctor, and doctors saw death all the time, but this was different. *Personal.*

'I just do. I wish I didn't, but…'

She laid her hand upon his arm, empathising with his pain. He looked so forlorn, so haunted by whatever the memory was. He'd been through something terrible. Perhaps he *did* know what he was talking about?

'I'm sorry.'

'What for?'

'For whoever you lost.'

'It was a long time ago. Besides, you haven't

lost anyone yet. We're nowhere near that. There's still hope. And time. You have to give the medicines time to work.'

Tasha let out a heavy sigh and turned back to look at her small charge, all the way across the room. 'Okay. You're right. *Again.*'

'And next time you feel the urge to consult Dr Internet, perhaps you might like to consult with me first?'

She crossed her heart. 'I promise.'

'Good.'

He was glad to go into surgery to assist in the removal of the goitre. He needed that intensity of concentration, the focus that only surgery could bring, after that moment with Tasha earlier on.

He'd had to reassure her, but he'd been worried, too. There'd been tears forming in her eyes and he hadn't wanted to see her cry. Not because crying women made him uncomfortable—he just didn't want to see *Tasha* cry.

He cared about her. Especially now that he'd been given a second chance to put things right in her life. And seeing her upset had upset him, too. It had felt as if it was *his* fault. That somehow he needed to put things right.

Having her stand before him with tears in her eyes and her bottom lip trembling had been like a flashback to all those years ago.

He couldn't have that. He *wouldn't.*

Now he had to think. Had to concentrate on the surgery. Make sure that he and his colleague both safely avoided the two laryngeal nerves which affected the vocal cords as they removed this goitre. They didn't want to paralyse this man's voice or his ability to breathe.

He'd felt paralysed. Briefly. Seeing her standing there, almost in tears. The surge of desire to make everything better for Tasha had startled him, and had made him realise just how much Tasha was beginning to mean to him already.

And that worried him. It had only been a few years since he had lost his wife and child. Was he having feelings he shouldn't have for another woman already?

Or was Tasha *just a friend*? As he kept telling himself she was.

This is all so complicated!

How many of his feelings were tied up in the past? His past with Tasha? Was it because he felt he owed her a debt? That he had to put things right? Or was this something different?

He felt her pull. She was a very beautiful woman. He'd done a double-take the first time she'd run onto his ward, then he'd spent hours staring at her face during that night in the tent in Mosa and wondered what it might be like to kiss her. The time they'd spent together since had been wonderful. Warm and refreshing. He looked forward to seeing her every day. Wanted to spend even more time with her. Wanted to be *with her.*

Guilt. That's what I'm feeling. Guilt that I might be moving on.

But it didn't mean he would forget Hannah, or his son. Of course he wouldn't. But was he ready for such a relationship? Was he reading too much into this in the first place?

He was sure Tasha felt something for him, too.

They were both just afraid. Afraid to put themselves out there and commit to it. Held back by fear.

He didn't want their relationship to be complicated, even if it was just as friends. He wanted—*needed*—this to be easy. Light. Enjoyable.

Quinn would never forget his wife and child, but if he wanted Tasha to be more open with him then he had to find the strength he had inside to let her know that she would be safe with him.

But she was so concerned about Abeje. So worried about her. Clearly she loved the child, and it was even clearer that they wouldn't stand a chance together unless Abeje lived.

He *had* to make her live.

He couldn't lose her.

Because if he did then he'd lose Tasha Kincaid as well.

Tasha spent the next couple of days teaching all day and going to visit Abeje in the evenings. The little girl looked so frail and small in her bed, her breathing sometimes ragged, sometimes not. She'd taken along the book of letters that the class had made and she spent each evening reading them out, convinced that even if Abeje wasn't conscious she would still absorb the positivity of the words, the good intentions, and that somehow they would help power her through this difficult battle.

Quinn often stopped by to speak to her, to update her on Abeje's condition and progress. He told her everything he could and she appreciated it that he didn't shield her from anything that might be construed as negative. He was open and forthcoming. Keen to make her understand his medical decisions and treatments, which she also appreciated.

When the end of that first week drew near, and the weekend stretched out ahead of them, he asked her if she'd like to go with him on a second trip to Mosa to check on the villagers and make sure that no one else had got sick.

She really wanted to go, but she glanced at Abeje in the bed. 'What about her? I don't like leaving her.'

'She's stable. We'll only be gone for the day. No overnight stay in a tent.'

'Are you taking the other two children back?'

'They're not ready yet. They're still sick.'

'Oh...' She wasn't sure if she really needed to go. What could she do? She wasn't a doctor here, or a nurse. And she'd only gone on that first trip because she knew Abeje's aunt. But then she thought about how nice it might be to get out of Ntembe and spend some more time with Quinn.

It had been nice that time they'd gone out for dinner, and she was enjoying their little chats each night, but he was always busy in the clinic and they didn't get to talk as much as she would have liked. Spending the day with him travelling to Mosa would be an opportunity to get to know him more.

She smiled. 'Okay. I will.'

'That's great!' He seemed really pleased. 'Maria and Rob will come too. I think it's important that the villagers see the same faces.'

The next day arrived quickly, and Tasha arrived portside to join the others in the truck to Mosa.

She got into the back of the truck with Quinn, as they'd offered to let Maria and Rob have the comfy seats this time. There was some equipment on the floor of the truck, along with boxes of tests and medications just in case, but Quinn was hopeful they wouldn't need any of it.

He banged his hand a couple of times on the back of the truck to indicate to Rob, who was driving, that they were ready to go, and the truck began to pull away from the dock.

It was weird, at first, being in the back of the truck with Quinn. They only had each other to look at. That or the road behind them, covered as they were by a khaki-green material hood.

He kept looking at her and smiling.

'What are you doing?'

'Looking at you.'

She felt her cheeks heat with colour. 'Why?'

She still felt it. The disbelief that he might be interested in her. That Quinn Shapiro would look at her with any interest that wasn't full of ridicule. Her young girl insecurities were still there, trying to hold her back.

'I'm just trying to decide if you'd agree to come out on a date with me.'

A date? Her heart raced at the idea. Thrilled that he'd suggested it, but also wary, she was unable to meet his gaze as her mind raced over possible outcomes at a mile a minute.

This man hurt you once! Don't you forget that!

Yes, he had, but that had been so long ago. They'd been children! A part of her really wanted to say yes…but what he had done before hadn't just hurt her for a short while. It had devastated her. Floored her for weeks, months.

She'd made a lot of her life choices because of this man. Choosing to become a doctor because she'd wanted the same things as him. Choosing to be *like him* because if she couldn't go out with him then she'd at least be experiencing the same world and hopes and dreams.

She couldn't just forget all that. It was such a huge part of her childhood. And choosing to be a doctor had led to one of the most disturbing episodes of her life—one that had overshadowed the humiliation he had put her through. She had questioned who she was. Whether she needed to be punished. She had had to change her entire life.

Besides, what if she did give in to his suggestion and it all went wrong and they ruined this friendship they were building? What if they had a great big falling-out and he devastated her again? And what was the point in dating him when he was going to leave in three weeks' time?

I'm always being left behind.

Her parents, Quinn, Simon.

She wanted to say yes, she *would* go on a date with him. She wanted to with all her heart. But they had a timeline working against them.

'Is that such a good idea?'

He sighed. 'I know…but don't you feel it? Our connection? It's more than just our history. I'm sure of it.'

The truck rattled them around as the tyres hit divots and potholes, but no matter how hard it shook them they still maintained eye contact.

'I'd be a liar if I said no.'

'So I'm not imagining it?'

Tasha smiled. 'No. You're not.'

'You can call us crazy, if you want. I don't mind. But I'd really like to spend more time with you, Tasha. Time that's meant for you and me. For *us*.'

She wanted it. She dearly wanted it. But *was* it crazy to do such a thing? Reckless? He would leave in three weeks. She would be left behind. Again! He'd sail off to Madagascar and not come back for months. She was only contracted for four more months in Ntembe. She could be gone by the time the *Serendipity* sailed back into port.

She was *so* tempted. Something about this man pulled her in. She couldn't help it any more than a moth could prevent itself from flying into the light. She knew it would probably all end in tears—mostly hers—but she still felt she wanted to take that chance. Just to see what would happen between them.

She felt helpless. As if she had no strength to resist him.

I loved him so much once...

He'd broken her heart before. Could she get involved with him knowing it might happen again? Or perhaps knowing there was a time limit on the relationship would help her cope with it better? Make her grateful for the magic times they might have? Cherish the memories of three weeks?

This was her opportunity to see if her childhood wishes were a possibility! A chance to see if she and Quinn would *work*. She wasn't a tearful thirteen-year-old any more. She was a grown woman, with life experience, and so far she'd survived all that life had thrown at her.

Why not this?

Why not have fun?

She'd survive again, wouldn't she…?

'No.'

His hopeful face dropped. 'No?'

She nodded. 'I want to… I do. It's just…'

He frowned. 'Just what?'

'Just that I think it's best we see each other as friends. Go out as friends and nothing more. There's too much water under the bridge.'

He looked disappointed. He leant forward, his

elbows on his knees, and stared out through the back of the truck.

Tasha watched him, feeling terrible but knowing she had done the right thing. The right thing to protect her heart.

The people of Mosa cheered to see them return. They wanted news on the two children who had been taken back to the ship, so Quinn filled them in on that. Then they gave the villagers a secondary check-up and no one else had succumbed to a bite from a mosquito, so it looked as if the villagers were in the clear.

Ada and some of the other women banded together and presented them with a meal of *bobotie*—spiced minced lamb with an egg topping.

And later, as Tasha was helping pack up the truck, Quinn came over to her and draped something around her neck. She stopped to look at it. It was a necklace, made with string and small pebbles that had been painted in bright rainbow colours. It was beautiful.

'Oh! That's gorgeous, thank you.'

She was surprised. After she'd turned him down in the truck he had barely said a word. So the fact that he had brought her something so beautiful made her see just how much he valued her despite her saying no.

'Ada said that the people here give each other these necklaces as a sign of friendship. To show that they will always be friends, no matter what.'

She fingered the small stones. They were tiny. Such work must have gone into each one to bore a hole for the string and then paint them in the array of colours…

'I love it, thank you.' She looked up at him, smiling, glad that her refusal had not made everything awkward. And he stood in front of her, close, their bodies almost touching. He stared at her for a long moment and her pulse raced under his close scrutiny.

She gazed at his mouth. His lips. She looked back into his eyes. She'd once dreamed of that first kiss. What it would feel like. His lips touching hers.

He reached up to tuck a stray curl behind her ear and she had to look away. Embarrassed and hot with the attention.

'Are you two gonna help? Or stare into each other's eyes all day?' joked Rob, interrupting their moment as he dropped a crate of meds back into the truck.

Quinn smiled at her, and then stepped back to get out of Rob's way. 'We'll help.'

She could breathe again!

She stepped back too, feeling her heart thudding, her pulse racing, her face burning with heat and desire.

These next three weeks are going to be intense.

Back in Ntembe, Tasha found she was living on her nerves. But in a good way. She looked forward to going to the ship to visit Abeje, knowing that Quinn would be there, too, exchanging glances and secret smiles with her. She might have agreed to just friendship, but it was a friendship unlike any she had ever experienced before.

There was heat between them. She felt it. She

knew he did, too. But he was respecting her choice, which she was glad about—even if she *did* keep dreaming about being in his arms at night.

It was like being thirteen again. But this time Quinn's reactions to her weren't just in her imagination. They were real.

And then on one of her visits he asked if she would like to go out for dinner.

'Just friends.' He smiled.

She nodded, almost too shy to speak, her heart thudding away like a thousand stampeding wildebeests. Dinner with Quinn would be very nice. And probably safe, too. Her on one side of a table, him on the other. Good food. Maybe some wine. Conversation. Moonlight.

He turned up at her door dressed in casual dark trousers and a white shirt that showed his tan to perfection. In his hand was a small posy of flowers. Where he'd got them from, she had no idea, but they were very beautiful.

'Are they *wild* flowers?'

He nodded, smiling.

'How did you get them?' She lifted them to her nose to inhale their scent—sweet and fragrant.

'You'd be amazed at what you can buy at a busy port.'

She raised an eyebrow. 'I'm sure.'

Quinn laughed. 'Are you ready?'

'Where are we going? You didn't say.'

'Somewhere special. Trust me.' He looked her up and down. 'You look very beautiful.'

She blushed, inordinately pleased at his compliment. But she told herself to put it into perspective. He was just being kind and polite. What man *didn't* say a woman looked nice when they'd both made an effort to go out somewhere together? Just because Quinn had said it, it didn't mean anything. They were just friends.

Me and Quinn....friends. I would never have believed it.

He escorted her out to his car, which looked like a jigsaw: different coloured panels everywhere. Nothing matching. A real rust-bucket.

'I know it's not a stretch limousine...'

She smiled. 'You couldn't buy one of those at the port?' she joked.

'They were all sold out.'

He opened the passenger door for her and she looked in at the familiar bursts of foam sticking out of the seat covers. It seemed such a long time ago that he'd taken her out to The Coffee Bean that night.

She'd not felt this happy for a long time, and she touched the pebble necklace at her throat with nerves. She'd wanted to wear it tonight. For him. To show that she appreciated his gesture. That they were both trying, here.

She laughed when the engine didn't start. 'Should I call for a mechanic?'

He looked at her a little bemused. 'Give it one more chance. All she needs is a little love and patience.'

'Don't we all?'

And then, on the fifth attempt, the engine roared into life, sounding as if it might conk out again at any moment.

'Are you sure we're going to make it home later?'

'I'll give you a piggy-back if I have to.'

Putting the car into first gear, he drove them away from Ntembe, kangarooing every now and again, before steering them down the main road and then taking a dusty side track that led them up a hill, signposted 'The Heights'.

The road was long and winding, skimming the edge of the mountain, providing them with terrifically scary views, and just before the top, where it levelled out, there was a small building, lit with dangling white lamps, with a small terrace that gave great views out to the sea.

She'd never known about this. Never seen it before. 'What *is* this place?'

'The Heights restaurant. An ex-patient owns it.'

'Wow!' It was all she could say.

The terrace was filled with intimate little tables for two, white tablecloths covering each one. There were candles and lamps, small potted plants, and on each table a single flower in a tall, thin glass vase.

Quinn got out and opened the car door for her, and she heard guitar music playing from speakers as she stepped out in her long maxi-dress.

The maître d'—a young, well-presented man in a black shirt and bow tie—escorted them to a table on the terrace.

'Thank you.' She sat down, smiling, and accepted the menu that he proffered. It was printed in the most elegant script, and it surprised her to find a place of such class and distinction in a part of Africa she'd always believed to be deprived.

'Tonight's specials are the *liboké de poisson* and our fishball stew.'

She frowned. 'What was the first one?'

The maître d' smiled. 'The *liboké de poisson* is our fish of the day, wrapped in banana leaves and baked.'

Mmm. Sounds wonderful.

Tasha thanked him and, as if he could read their minds and knew that they needed to chat and discuss life before choosing their food, the maître d' slunk away almost as if by magic.

She smiled at Quinn over her menu. 'How did you find this place?'

'I actually discovered it on one of my first trips here. One of the doctors who'd volunteered on the ship was retiring, and we all came here in a group of about forty. We took over the whole restaurant, and I remember it because the food and the views were just so amazing. Later the guy who owns it came to us for a procedure.'

'Is everyone on the *Serendipity* a volunteer?'

'A lot of them, yes.'

'Are you?'

'No, I've been there too long.' He smiled. 'What would you like to drink?'

'I'll have a dry white wine, please.'

'Sounds great. I'll join you.'

The maître d' appeared and Quinn gave their order, and they both soon had their glasses filled with the house special.

The staff came and went like culinary ghosts.

'It's just so beautiful up here,' she said, gazing out at the bay far below, where vessels bobbed on the water like rubber ducks.

It wasn't chilly. The night was perfect. They could see the *Serendipity*, and all the other boats and ships docked in port. There were the lights of Ntembe, and beyond that the port, and the vast stretch of water that was the Mozambique Channel. All glittering in the moonlight.

'It's peaceful up here, too. Makes you feel that you have no hardships. That there's nothing to worry about. It's hard to imagine that there are hundreds of people down there, all living their lives, going about their business, unaware that we're looking down on them from above.'

A waiter came and took their food order.

'It's important to get away from things sometimes,' Quinn said. 'The pressures of life and living. Escapism is good every now and again.'

Tasha knew about escaping. She'd done it to survive. But there was a difference between escaping physically and escaping mentally. Once something was inside your head—fear, guilt, shame—you couldn't escape that no matter where you went. You took it with you.

Escaping to a different place, going for a nice

meal, like tonight, or going on holiday to Bali or Bora Bora, or wherever, was just window dressing. Wherever you chose to go it wouldn't help at all unless you got everything right in your head. You could choose to try not to think about something for a while—read a book, watch a movie, have time out with friends or a loved one—but it would always be waiting for you. Lurking in the dark recesses of your mind. Ready to cause trouble and anguish once again.

'It is. Sometimes we need to pretend that everything's okay and that we have nothing to worry about.'

He smiled and raised his glass to her in a toast. 'Here's to having nothing to worry about.'

She clinked his glass with her own and took a sip of wine. It was deliciously fruity. 'And here's to Abeje getting better.'

He clinked her glass. 'To Abeje. And every other patient on the ship tonight.'

'We never do stop worrying, though, do we? You have patients you must think about constantly, and I have students who are never far from my mind.'

Quinn nodded. 'Are there *any* jobs, do you think, in which people can truly switch off from work the second they leave?'

She thought about it for a moment, her mind reaching for possibilities before throwing them away. 'I really don't know.'

He smiled at her. 'It's just human nature, I guess.'

'But working with children, like you and I both do, isn't that the hardest?'

She wondered if he'd ever experienced what she had. If he'd ever had to make a choice over someone's life, Decided who to treat first, knowing that the one you left till second might die because of that decision?

'It can be. There have been times when I have truly not wanted to be a doctor. The knowledge it gives you is powerful, but when there's nothing to be done it can be… At times like that I wish I could walk away. But I made an oath and I meant it.'

She'd made that oath, too.

Once.

And she *had* walked away.

What does that make me? Am I a coward? Or should I just never have been a doctor in the first place?

She gazed down at the sheer white tablecloth, adjusted her cutlery slightly. Sipped her wine. Remembering.

Remembering what she'd done.

CHAPTER FIVE

THEIR WAITER BROUGHT them a platter of seafood—oysters, crab, shrimp, calamari—served with scalloped potatoes, fresh crusty bread and curls of butter, the aromas of which, caused their mouths to salivate in anticipation.

As other guests arrived and the restaurant began to fill up they chatted pleasantly over their meal.

Tasha was aware that as it got darker Quinn's eyes looked even more devilish, twinkling in the low lantern light. He smiled a lot, and he was a good listener as she told him some of her teaching stories.

'So, how long have you been a teacher?' he asked.

'Oh, not that long,' she answered without thinking, his easy-going nature having made her let down her guard.

'So what did you do when you left school?'

Oh.

She shrugged. 'This and that. I kind of drifted,' she lied, hating herself for telling him untruths, but not sure she could tell him everything.

How would he look at her if she did? She'd *quit* being a doctor! She'd made that oath that was so important to him and then she'd walked away. She'd lost a child. A whole *life*. Because of making the wrong choice. Could she tell him *that*?

No. Not when she was enjoying spending time with him. He would look at her differently. View her differently. Here he was in Africa, saving lives, giving medicine to those who had none.

He gave his all here. She could see that. Even if she *did* get frustrated at the level of response Abeje was showing. And she liked being a success in his eyes. It was an image she wanted to maintain—especially with him.

That earlier part of her life was something that

she found shameful, and she didn't feel comfortable enough with him yet to tell him the truth. She would have to keep that to herself until he left. And each and every time she saw him after that. If they got the chance.

'What about you? Did you keep in touch with Dexter?'

He smiled at the name. 'Dexter Green…now *that's* a name I haven't thought of for a while. I did for a bit. But he went off to one uni and I went off to another. You know how it is—you lose touch, sometimes.'

'I wonder what he ended up doing?'

'I think he was a sports journalist, last I heard.' He patted his mouth with a napkin. 'Do you keep in touch with any of the kids from the children's home?'

She shook her head. 'No. The day I left I cut every tie.'

'You must have been lonely.'

'I had a new foster family to get to know.'

He frowned and reached out to take her hand, gave it a reassuring squeeze. 'I'm sorry you didn't have a great start in life. But look at you now. In Africa, doing a job that you love, living the dream…'

She smiled back, aware of the sensations as he touched her. Stroked the back of her hand with his thumb. It was a simple gesture, but intimate. One that was sending fireworks of frenzy zipping around her body, making her high on adrenaline. She couldn't help but stare at their hands interlocked upon the tablecloth.

'Are you finished with your plates?'

Their waiter had come to take the platter away. They thanked him, told him it had been delicious, and he magicked away their used crockery with a smile of satisfaction upon his face.

'It *is* your dream? Teaching?' He was looking at her carefully. Trying to read the emotions rushing across her face.

'Of course. It's just…'

'What?'

'Abeje getting so sick…it's thrown me.'

'Children get sick.' His eyes darkened.

'Yes, but if we were back in England she'd

have a cold or tonsillitis. This is *malaria.* It could kill her.'

He squeezed her fingers more reassuringly.

Then their waiter came back to their table. 'Excuse me, sir. You're Dr Shapiro?'

'Yes?'

'There's an urgent telephone call for you inside.'

An urgent call. Was it Abeje? Suddenly the food in Tasha's stomach sat heavily. Sickeningly.

Quinn glanced at her apologetically. 'Excuse me.' He dabbed his mouth once again with the napkin and got up.

She watched him go, weaving his way through the tables, following the waiter to the phone.

When he was gone she pulled her hand back towards herself and thought about what she was feeling. Quinn was making her question herself and she was feeling very disconcerted. *Was* she living her dream? Or was she just in her fall-back position of teaching?

She *missed* medicine, but she wasn't certain she was strong enough to go back to doing it. Perhaps there was a branch of medicine she could be in that wouldn't be so upsetting? Dermatology? Ear, nose and throat? But she knew instinctively that any of these options also carried risks. No matter where she went or what she chose she would always face heartbreaking cases.

And now she was here. With Quinn. Closer to him than she had ever believed possible.

He wasn't gone long. Just a few minutes. He came back into view, striding to their table, his face sombre.

He stood by her side. 'I'm sorry to cut our date short, but we have to go.'

She stood up, feeling nauseous and suspecting she already knew the answer to her question but having to ask anyway. 'Is something wrong?'

He nodded, and looked as if he was deciding about whether to tell her the next part or not.

'It's Abeje. She's taken a turn for the worse.'

Quinn got them back to the ship in less than twenty minutes, but it was the longest twenty minutes of Tasha's life so far. All she could imagine was getting on board and hearing those terrible words. The words she couldn't bear to hear.

During the drive back she'd bombarded Quinn with questions.

'What did they say, exactly?'

'That she's spiked a high fever and that her urine output has slowed.'

'How high a fever?'

'They didn't say.'

'Well, was it over a hundred?'

'He didn't say.'

'Well, when he said her output had slowed, did he say how much? How many millilitres an hour is she producing? How full was her bag?'

'He didn't say.'

She'd got so frustrated with him! So angry.

'When did she last have a kidney function test?'

'A few hours ago.'

'What were the results?'

'I wasn't there. I was seeing to other patients, It'll be in her notes.'

If the kidneys failed it would be a slippery slope from there. All her organs would shut down. She'd fall into a coma.

She might die.

She'd seen it happen before. The kidneys were often the barometer of the body. You watched the kidneys like a hawk.

Not being able to see Abeje's most recent notes, not to have them in her hands…

Why did I agree to this date? If I hadn't said yes we'd be there right now!

Tasha had felt as if she wanted to throw up. Adrenaline firing, her heart hammering, her throat feeling tight and closed. She had even shivered as Quinn raced them back down that hill towards Ntembe port.

I can't lose her! She can't die!

She had to lift up her skirt to run up the gangplank after Quinn, whose massive stride seemed to take no effort at all, and they burst into the clinic together and headed straight for Abeje's bedside.

She looked listless and clammy, her breathing irregular.

'Let's get her on oxygen right now, and I want a full blood screen, asap!' Quinn ordered, grabbing the stethoscope from Rob's neck and listening to Abeje's breathing and heartbeat. 'Heart sounds strong.'

Tasha grabbed the notes from the end of the bed and ran her gaze over all the figures, interpreting what she saw. The kidney function tests seemed okay. The bottom end of normal, but still within the normal range.

Why had Quinn not double-checked this? *Why* hadn't he been concerned?

'Heart-rate's good.'

She had to grab on to any strands of hope she could.

She tried to keep out of the way, but the desire to rush forward and grab the stethoscope from his hands, push him out of the way and tend to Abeje herself, was overwhelming. Instead she hung the notes back on the edge of the bed and backed off, grabbing the counter, grounding herself and telling herself that she couldn't do that. She had no right to practice medicine.

All she could do was hold that counter, concentrate on the feel of it in her hands, as Quinn and Rob tended to Abeje.

The oxygen seemed to be helping.

'SATs are back up to ninety-five.'

'Respirations are at twenty-two.'

Quinn ordered medication and wrote down all his observations on Abeje's chart.

'What's happening now?' Tasha asked.

'We've got to wait and see if her fever comes down.'

'That's *it*? Wait and see?'

Surely there was more they could do? Not that she could think of anything herself.

'It's all we *can* do. I've given her meds and full oxygen. We've taken bloods to check the status of her levels. Until those results come back there's nothing more we can do.'

'There must be *something*!' She raced to the side of Abeje's bed and grabbed the little girl's hand. 'We can't just leave her to…'

'To what?' Quinn looked at her strangely.

She stared at Abeje's face. So serene. So peaceful. She almost looked as she was…

Tasha closed her eyes, wincing. She couldn't think that. She *couldn't*! 'I can't lose her.'

'We're not at that point. No way near.' He laid a hand on her shoulder, then knelt by her side and made her look at him. 'Hey, she's okay at the moment. Stable.'

'But critical. That's the bit you're not saying, isn't it? I read the notes.'

He looked away, guiltily.

She turned back to Abeje. Thinking of how far she'd come. Of all that she had survived. 'Do you know what her name means?'

'Abeje? No. I don't.'

'It means *We asked to have this child.*' Tasha turned to Quinn, tears in her eyes. 'She was wanted, Quinn. She was *wanted*! A precious first child! She wasn't meant to be an orphan! She wasn't meant to be in a children's home, all alone with no one to care for her.'

'But she *does* have people caring for her. She has us. She has *you.*'

Tasha wiped away a tear that had escaped her eye and trickled down her cheek in a lonely waterfall. 'What if I'm not strong enough?'

He frowned, lines furrowing his brow. 'Why wouldn't you be strong enough?'

She gazed at him, tears blurring her vision. 'I'm not. I'm *not*!'

She began to cry. Big, snotty sobs—proper, ugly crying—as she thought about all that Abeje had been through and *still* had to go through. Life was unfair. Seemingly all the *good* people—her, Abeje—who deserved to have a *good* life, were given traumatic ones instead. Their lives filled with heartache and pain.

Abeje wasn't even a teenager yet and she'd had both parents die, ended up in an orphanage with almost no hope of being adopted and now she was fighting for her life! Tasha thought *she'd* had it bad as a child, but it was nothing compared to this! She'd never been struck down by a terrible illness. The worst she'd had was the flu.

Why? It made no sense to her at all.

Quinn slipped his hand into hers. 'Come with me.'

'What? No. I can't leave her.'

'Tasha. Come with me. Please.'

She looked up at him, sniffing, not caring how she looked, wondering why he wanted her to go with him. 'But, Abeje—'

'Abeje will be fine for a moment. Please. Come with me.'

He looked so determined. So certain. So sure.

Feeling the need to latch on to someone strong, she got up and allowed him to lead her out of the ward and along another corridor. They went down a flight of stairs and he led them to what looked like a maternity ward. There were about five women on the ward. All new mothers. Two of them had their babies in their arms and were breastfeeding.

Tasha frowned, confused. 'What are we doing here?'

'I want you to look at these women. At these mothers.'

She frowned. 'Why?'

'Because you need to know how strong you are.'

She shook her head. 'I don't get it…'

He took her hand and gestured at the women on the ward.

'Each of these women thought that they weren't strong enough to carry on. They were exhausted and spent. And each time they thought they couldn't handle another second, another contraction, we told them that they had to. Because they did. If they didn't find that strength—if they chose to stop—something terrible might have happened. So they pushed. And pushed. And when they thought they couldn't push any more we told them to hang in there. That they could. That they were strong. They kept on because those babies in their arms, those children in their care, are the most important thing in the world and they *had* to do it. Tasha, you're a remarkable young woman. You overcame a difficult start in life and you're here, alone, in a developing country, fighting to improve the lives of children. Don't you *see* how strong you are?'

'I'm not a mother.'

'Mothers aren't necessarily the women who give birth to a child, but those who love them.'

She frowned, thinking. 'Like the woman who fostered me?'

He nodded. 'Yes. She didn't give birth to you, but I bet she loved and cared for you like she had.'

It was true. Tasha had even called her 'Mum'. Still did to this day. It had been one of the most surprising events of her life, finding a home. People to care for her. Love her. She'd thought all her chances were gone.

'You're telling me I can *do* this?'

His voice was soft and gentle. 'I'm telling you, you can do this.'

He reached up to stroke her face, the backs of his fingers tracing the line of her jaw, his gaze focused on her lips.

She smiled hesitantly, feeling his arms come around her body and hold her close. She soaked up his strength. His belief in her.

Staring at him, this close, she could almost barely breathe. Time stopped. The air felt thick with tension. She looked at his mouth. The mouth she had once dreamed of kissing. The mouth that belonged to the man she had once loved so much her heart had almost broken in two. She could feel it. Wanted to belong to him again.

He lowered his head towards hers.

He was going to kiss her.

She could protest. She could pull away. She could tell him no.

But she didn't want to.

Tasha closed her eyes and allowed her lips to meet his.

Quinn wished they could stay like that for hours. Tasha in his arms, her body against his. The feel of her, the scent of her hair, her perfume… It was a heady mix.

He hated the fact that she'd got so upset. He'd felt it. Her pain. Her fear of losing the child. And he'd known he had to give her hope. Because there still *was* hope. For both of them.

What he'd said was true. Women *were* infinitely stronger than men—mentally, physically and emotionally. They had greater depths to dig from.

Look at Hannah and the way she'd coped with everything thrown at her. She'd had cancer and she had done her level best to protect him from the pain she was in as she strove to grow their child, tried to give him life.

She'd tried to protect him as well as their son, whilst ignoring her own welfare. Had tried to carry on with life as if everything was normal. She had even made plans for their future, as if she'd believed she had one.

And he'd gone along with it—hoping and praying that she would be there with him to change nappies and do midnight feeds and watch their child take his first steps. Had he blinded himself? Deliberately made himself naïve to what was going on?

Desperate people made desperate decisions.

Hannah had fought till the bitter end, knowing that every minute their son stayed in the womb was an extra chance that he would survive. She had been utterly unselfish, staying alive for their son for as long as she could, fighting for every breath just as he had done.

And now he found himself with yet another strong woman.

Tasha had no idea of the depths of her strength.

She was frightened, and he understood that, but once she pushed past that fear she would realise just how much she had inside her still, in order to fight and to keep on fighting.

That was why he had brought her down to this ward. Because being here helped him. Reminded him of what life was all about. Because it wasn't about death. It was about life. And living.

Being here also hurt him. Seeing these mothers holding their babies in a way Hannah had never got the chance to do. Seeing these full-term babies when his own had been so small. But he could push past that pain because Tasha was worth it. She needed to see. Needed to understand.

And now had stood there kissing her.

Kissing a woman who wasn't his wife.

It should have felt awful. Treasonous. An act of betrayal.

And it did.

But it also felt amazing and right. And something about Tasha being in his arms, about Tasha being the woman he was kissing, seemed to be a full circle completing itself.

He hadn't kissed her because he felt he owed it to her. He hadn't kissed her to make up for what he had done to her as a teenager. He'd kissed her because he'd needed to. Wanted to.

And the crevasse in his heart was beginning to close.

No one had ever said life was going to be easy. He'd been through the worst thing anyone could ever experience—the loss of his wife and his baby—and yet he was still here. Still breathing. Still putting one foot in front of the other.

He knew Tasha could do it, too. Even if he had to hold her hand.

He liked doing that. Touching her. Holding her. He drew comfort from it—a comfort that he hadn't realised he'd been missing.

Tasha gave him a strength that he'd forgotten about. Gave him the need to care about someone. The need to be close to another human being.

It was not just about friendship, though that was very nice. It was about having that special connection. Something deeper, more primal than friendship. A vulnerability. That was what you got when you opened up your heart and let someone in.

'Are you ready to go back up?' he asked her, staring into her deep blue eyes.

'One more minute,' she replied, and laid her head soothingly against his chest.

Tasha sat beside Abeje's bed, straight of back and rigid of jaw, telling herself sternly that she could *do* this. Quinn believed in her. All she had to do was believe in herself. Sit by Abeje's bedside and not freak out.

Abeje was still breathing. Still alive.

The worst had not happened. And it might never happen. She had to believe that.

She cast her mind back to how she'd freaked out like that once before. That day she'd quit being a doctor. She'd sunk to the hospital floor, knowing she was responsible for the death of a child, staring at the tiles, wondering how on earth she was going to be able to call the parents in the middle of the night and tell them they needed to come in.

Her hands had visibly shaken as she'd picked up the phone, she'd even misdialled twice, her fingers had trembled so much, and then there had been that awful moment when she'd heard the mother, at the other end of the line, picking up even before the second ring and saying hello.

Her mouth had gone so dry. Her heart had thudded dully in her chest—an ever-present reminder that even though *her* heart could still beat, this woman's daughter's could not. Did not.

This woman's daughter was lying in a secluded bay, a white sheet pulled over her face.

How could she speak? How could she find the words that must be said?

The mother had begun to sound panicked.

'Hello? Is there anyone there?'

There was just a blank after that. She wasn't sure what she'd done in the time from that phone call to the time the parents arrived, dishevelled and red-eyed, at just after three a.m.

The Family Room had been small. Two sofas,

facing each other. A small table in between with a vase of fake flowers and a box of man-sized tissues. There'd been an odd stain on one of the cushions and a frankly pallid painting of a beach scene on the wall.

The parents had looked at her anxiously, wringing their hands, their faces pale.

'What's happened? How's Maddie?'

'I'm sorry...' she'd begun, and the parents had collapsed in on themselves even before she'd got to the end of her sentence.

It had been horrific to witness.

She'd delivered news like that before and had always managed to maintain a professional distance. Stating the facts clearly, telling the family that she was sorry and then leaving them to have some privacy whilst they mourned. Going back in later, after a respectable amount of time, to ask if they'd like to see their loved one?

But not that time.

The rawness of those parents' grief, the keening sound of the mother as she'd collapsed against her husband, the guilt that she'd felt, had ripped Tasha's heart in two.

I did this. It's my fault. Maddie shouldn't have died.

She'd fled the room, pulled off her lanyard and thrown it to the floor. Stalked to her locker, taken her things and walked out. Never to return.

Her mobile phone had rung almost non-stop, Simon's name flashing up constantly. Her email inbox had overflowed, but she'd answered nothing.

There'd been an investigation—of course there had. And the coroner had said that no one was to blame for the tragedy—certainly not Dr Tasha Kincaid, who'd had to make an agonising decision in the middle of a busy nightshift on call. But that hadn't made her feel any better. She'd still felt to blame and the sound of Maddie's mother's crying and wailing had woken her most nights.

Was Quinn right? *Did* she have the strength to get through this?

Abeje's still alive. That's what I have to cling on to.

But the insidious thought remained that the tables might soon be turned. That Tasha would not be the doctor delivering the bad news but instead the person taken into a family room and having Quinn in front of her saying, *I'm sorry...*

Quinn—whom she'd kissed. And not as a friend.

What did it all mean?

She stared hard at Abeje in her hospital bed, willing her to get better.

'I've brought you some tea and toast.'

Tasha had slept in the chair next to Abeje's bed all night, and now it was morning. The fever had come down, and the child's condition was stable once again. But Tasha looked crumpled and exhausted.

She took it from him, her face smiling with gratitude. 'Thanks.'

'You stayed?'

'I did.'

'We have temporary cots, you know. I could

have brought you one so that you didn't have to sleep in a chair.'

'Well, maybe next time.'

'She's improved a little. I think you might make it home tonight.'

'I have to teach today,' she said, stretching and wincing at a pain in her shoulder.

'Here—let me.' And he stood behind her and began to massage the knots out of her muscles.

She gave a little groan of pleasure and he tried his hardest not to replay that sound in his head. But he couldn't help it. His mind made him wonder what it would be like to hear her make different noises of pleasure.

Quickly he admonished himself. *Be a professional, Quinn! You're still at work.*

'That feels good,' she said. 'Were you up all night?'

'I got forty winks in the on-call room.'

'Lucky you.'

She could have joined me.

His body stirred at the thought of that, and he had to let go of her shoulders and walk round to the other side of the bed to create some distance, hoping she didn't notice that he might look a little flushed.

Where were all these thoughts coming from? Okay, so they'd kissed once. And it had been amazing. But what had it really meant? Had he just been comforting her? Or had he truly allowed his desires to take over? He'd begun to believe he would never desire another woman ever again, so what was happening to him?

She smiled her thanks and then picked up a triangle of buttered toast. 'Mmm. Lovely.'

'Abeje's doing well. Her fever broke during the night. And the two kids from Mosa are doing well, too.'

'That's great. Have you got to work today?'

He nodded.

'Shame. I would have liked to be able to show you my class of kids and how wonderful they are.'

'Maybe I could come over during my lunch break?'

She beamed. 'That would be great! Look, thanks

for this, but I'd better get back and change. Have a quick shower.'

'Of course. I'll see you later?'

'I'll look forward to it.'

She took a quick sip of her tea and then bolted, and when she'd gone, leaving sweet perfume in her wake, he realised just how much he was missing her already.

He liked having her around. She was sweet and caring and loving. Tasha had a big heart. She always had. She fell in love easily.

Was he capable of the same thing?

He woke with a start, the lingering effects of his bad dream ebbing from his mind as he blinked his eyes to clear them of sleep and tried to slow his racing heart.

He'd only meant to have a power nap, and normally he didn't dream—or if he did he didn't remember. But this one had been fierce in its imagery.

He'd been with his wife, Hannah. She'd been lying in bed, her hands protectively wrapped around her stomach. He'd been kneeling beside her, talking to the baby in her belly, telling him about how much he was already loved. But when he'd finished—when he'd looked up to smile at Hannah—it wasn't her any more but Tasha, and she'd been holding Abeje in her arms, crying, screaming at him to save her!

'Save my child! You have to save my child!'

Quinn rubbed at his eyes and stood up from the bed in the on-call room, stretching. The dream had unsettled him. But for what reason he wasn't sure. Because Hannah had become Tasha? Because he was worrying about Abeje? Or was it more to do with how connected to Abeje Tasha was?

He knew he shouldn't be worrying about this. He was impressed by her dedication as Abeje's teacher. Clearly she cared for the children in her class. and that was a good thing. But…

But what?

What if it all goes wrong and I can't save her?

No doctor liked to think the worst, but sometimes you had to consider your course of action.

Malaria was contentious. Tricky. You never knew how people were going to react to the meds. Sometimes it came down to how well they'd been *before* they'd got infected, but they'd done a full work-up on Abeje and hadn't found anything else wrong.

Quinn ran his fingers through his hair and then quickly brushed his teeth. It was nearly time for him to go and see Tasha. He said he'd pop down to the school to meet the other kids.

But maybe he shouldn't? Maybe he was getting too deeply involved here?

He liked Tasha. Immensely. He couldn't deny it and he'd like their relationship to go further. But…

Perhaps I'm getting cold feet?

Did he really want to get into another relationship? Another relationship in which the welfare of a child was of primary significance? Did he need that complication? No one could know if Abeje would survive this and he feared Tasha's reaction if she didn't.

Tasha needed to get some space. She needed to

take a step back. She wasn't Abeje's mother—she'd said it herself. Perhaps he needed to help her decide just who she was to the child? She could go either way, but then he'd know. Know what he was up against.

He hated not knowing—the blind naivety that believed everything should be all right as long as they remained positive.

His reflection stared back at him from the small shaving mirror and he let out a sigh, feeling terrible for the thoughts he was having. Who was *he* to say who she should care for?

But he'd experienced the loss of a child and Tasha hadn't, and she had no idea of what it could do to a person. He needed to warn her, somehow. He needed to make her let go—because if she didn't she just might be devastated, and he wasn't sure he could deal with that, with being the cause of her pain once again.

Because he *would* be the cause, wouldn't he? If Abeje died then Tasha would think it was because *he* hadn't been able to save her, and he didn't want the blame.

He'd been blamed for a death before. Hannah's family, in their guilt, their grief, had taken it out on him, telling him that as a doctor he should have saved her. Should have fought to make her take the chemo and have a baby later!

'You should have made her take the chemo, Quinn! What kind of a husband are you?'

The accusation of their voices was still bitter in his mind.

He'd lost patients before—of course he had. All doctors had. But this case was different. Was personal because of Tasha. And he wasn't ready for that. Wasn't ready for the intense emotions that were already playing out between them.

He would fight and do his best for every patient, but Abeje had become a VIP. It was vital he didn't lose her.

Because he wasn't sure he could be witness to Tasha's collapse.

And to her blame.

It was scorching away from the air-conditioning of the boat. An oppressive heat that weighed as heavy as his fears. Despite it, he decided to walk to the school where Tasha taught. He felt he needed it—a little time to gain perspective on all that was happening. A little time to think of what he needed to say to her. That maybe he was rushing into a relationship he hadn't thought through properly. That maybe they ought to put the brakes on for a while—at least whilst Abeje was still sick.

I'm too close. I need to be Abeje's doctor, but I can't do that properly if I'm involved with Tasha.

All his patients deserved his utmost care, but he was beginning to feel as if Abeje should have *more*, somehow. His decisions and choices were being clouded by his feelings for her.

It felt good to walk through the port, where the fishermen were offloading their catches and wares. It was busy and vibrant and full of noisy life. A good reminder that outside of the confines of the boat, where he was generally surrounded by sick people, there were others living their lives as best they could.

There was happiness here, and warmth and

community. People *knew* one another, and as he passed through the crowds he was greeted often and frequently by broad, smiling faces.

He loved these people. He really did. They filled him with an energy and a purpose that he had never found elsewhere—not since Hannah, anyway. They were people with a genuine need…not like some of the people who would sometimes wander into A&E back home, complaining of a broken acrylic nail or a splinter, or something equally stupid.

Medical care here wasn't abused at all.

Perhaps I should have pushed Hannah more.

He'd kept his emotions contained after Hannah had died. And then, when he'd lost his son hours later, he'd bottled them up. It had been easier to retreat into a numbed state. His father, an ex-Marine, had raised him to believe that if he was to grow into a big, strong man then he would have to get control of the wobbly emotions he had inside him. That crying was for the weak.

Quinn wasn't sure that was true any more. He

wished he *could* cry sometimes. It might help to let the lid off the pressure cooker.

As he neared the school he could hear the children inside one class reading aloud from a book as one. He recognised the names of the characters and smiled, imagining Tasha standing at the front of the class, holding her book about wizards.

She must have seen him through a window, because suddenly she was leaning out of one, smiling happily and waving him over. 'Quinn! Come on in and I'll introduce you!'

He felt his heart lift at the sight of her beautiful face and gorgeous smile, and he smiled back and waved in return, feeling a cold lump inside his gut. He knew that he was about to hurt her. To do something he'd vowed not to do again. But he was doing it in the best interests of his patient and she would want that.

At least that was what he tried to tell himself.

She was energised. He could see that. She had to be a great teacher if she smiled like that all day long. Tasha was in a job that she loved and he could understand that. She made a perfect teacher. And she cared.

Inside, a sea of smiling faces awaited him.

'Everyone, I want you to say hello to Dr Shapiro, who works on the *Serendipity*—the hospital ship we visited a few days ago. Dr Shapiro is looking after Abeje.'

'Hi, Dr Shapiro!' the children all intoned, one or two waving from the front row.

'It's great to meet you all,' he said, smiling. 'Miss Tasha has told me all about you.'

They seemed happy about that, and Tasha stood beside him, beaming. 'We were reading, Quinn. Would you like to finish off the chapter before they all go out to lunch?'

'I'd love to!'

Anything to delay the inevitable.

He took the book from her and she pointed out where they'd got to. Her fingers brushed his and he felt that frisson he always felt when she touched him. He swallowed—hard.

'Okay, let's see how this goes…'

He began to read and the class listened intently.

Something special seemed to wrap itself around him as he stood reading at the front of the class. It was the way everyone was listening and reading along with him. The silence of their expectation as he tried to do special voices and vary his tone, giving it everything he could. It felt so good he wanted it to last for ever.

He had them all in the palm of his hand… rapt. And when he came to the end of the chapter and closed the book the classroom of children all looked up at him and began to clap appreciatively. He stood there, gave a slight bow, and looked at Tasha—who was also clapping.

Was this what it was like for her every day? To have *this?* He could see why she loved it. He'd adored every second.

'Okay, everyone. Put your books away and then I want you to line up by the door for lunch.'

The children all did as they were told and quietly, one by one, they lined up as instructed. Tasha stood by the door, waiting patiently for the last stragglers, and then she let them out, saying something kind to each one, thanking all the children for their efforts that morning.

When they were gone she closed the door and turned to him. 'Wow. I didn't know you could read like that!'

'Neither did I. It just...*happened*.'

'Well, I'm sure they'd love you to read to them from now on. I'll be out of a job!'

'No fear. I wouldn't have a clue what to do. I think I'll stick with doctoring.'

She smiled. 'I'm starving. Want to grab a bite to eat?'

'Sure.'

'Great!' She grabbed her bag from the back of her chair. 'And whilst we're queuing up for lunch you can tell me how Abeje is doing.'

They both purchased a small portion of stew that had been made with lamb and a variety of vegetables, served with some kind of wonderfully light dumpling that he'd never tasted before. He hadn't realised how hungry he was until the food was in front of him.

'How has she got on this morning?' asked Tasha.

'Pretty much the same, I have to say.'

Tasha sighed. 'It seems to be taking so *long*. I can't bear it—the not knowing.'

'She has one of the most aggressive strains of parasitical infection.'

'I know, but you gave her treatment for that. The two children from Mosa seem to be doing better than she is.' She let out a sigh. 'I'll come and sit with her again tonight. Look at her chart… see if there's something we haven't thought of.'

Quinn frowned, confused. 'Have you been researching on the internet again? I told you not to do that.'

She coloured slightly, stirred her stew. 'I couldn't help it.'

He stirred his own stew with his spoon, his appetite disappearing as he thought of how to voice his next words.

'Maybe you shouldn't come to the ship again.'

She looked up at him, questioning. 'Why?' A frown lined her brow.

'You need a break. You'll exhaust yourself this

way. Teaching for long hours, then spending all night by Abeje's bedside. You've got to look after yourself.'

'I'm not the one who's sick. She *needs* me. I have to be there for her. She has no one else fighting in her corner.'

He felt a little affronted by that. '*Doesn't* she? My team are doing everything they can. *I'm* doing everything I can. Can't you see that?'

'I know that—but it's not the same as having someone by your bed, holding your hand. Like a mother.'

'You're *not* her mother, though.'

Tasha put down her spoon and frowned at him. '*What?* One minute you're taking me to the maternity ward and showing me mothers, telling me that I'm *like* a mother, and now this about-face? Why are you being like this?'

Perhaps he *was* giving her mixed messages, but his thoughts about the situation were all over the place right now. He didn't want to have to give Tasha bad news. He didn't want to be that doctor who had to stand in front of someone and tell them their loved one had died. He couldn't do that to her.

'I'm just trying to look out for you.'

'Well, you don't have to. *I'm* not your concern. Abeje is.'

'But this isn't just about Abeje, is it? It's about *you.* You see yourself in her so you're trying to save her.'

'What's wrong with that?'

'An abandoned kid in a children's home—'

'Lots of my students are from the children's home.'

'But *they're* not the ones you can't tear yourself away from!' He looked away, feeling an anger that he hadn't known he had rising inside him. 'You need to take a step back.'

He could feel the pressure coming from her. The demand that he did not allow Abeje to deteriorate.

'You need to remember you're just her teacher. If anyone can save her it's me, not you, and you've got to allow me to do my job!'

Tasha stood up abruptly, her spoon clattering

to the floor as she threw her napkin on the table. ‘I can’t believe you’re saying this.’

Then she grabbed her bag, threw it over her shoulder and stormed away. Everyone else in the small dining room stared at him, wondering what he’d said to upset their favourite teacher. He hated the fact he’d made her angry. Hated the fact that he couldn’t make his mind up about what he wanted her to be. Who she needed to be. How she was making him feel.

Were those thoughts more about *his* feelings than *hers?*

He patted his mouth with a napkin and pushed his plate away.

CHAPTER SIX

TASHA STOOD OUTSIDE the school building fuming. How *dared* he say such things to her? What right did he have? He didn't *know* her. Not really. He had no idea of all that she'd been through. Or what she was capable of.

You're not her mother....

No. She wasn't. But mothers weren't just the women that gave birth to a child. *He'd* been the one to tell her that! Mothers were created through love. Created by the bond of a woman who cared for a child as if it were their own. Which was how she felt about Abeje.

Abeje had no one else.

Tasha couldn't help but recall those long, lonely nights, sitting in her bed at the children's home, wondering if life would ever get better. Her back against the wall, her knees tucked up against her chest, she had stared out of her open curtains and wondered if there was anyone out there who would care and love for her the way she wanted. With the intensity of love that would make them take a bullet for her. If there might be someone out there who would love her so much that they would be devastated if anything happened to her.

She'd had no one else.

She'd felt surplus to requirements. An overspill in a children's home already fit to bursting with lost children. But she'd grown up, and now she'd come here, and she'd met all these kids, and Abeje had found a way into her heart.

Abeje wanted to be a doctor, too. They were so similar! She couldn't help that any more than she could help her need to breathe. *She* could make that girl feel someone cared. And having Quinn tell her to back off was just way out of line!

She couldn't tell her heart just to switch off. Because if she could she'd probably still be a doctor. She wouldn't have nightmares. She wouldn't be feeling all sorts of emotions that she didn't want.

She'd be happy.

Not standing here with tears in her eyes.

She looked up as the school door opened and Quinn stepped out, his magnificent form filling the doorway. He scanned the play area, looking for her.

Wiping her eyes, she began to walk away.

'Tasha! Wait!'

'I don't want to talk to you, Quinn!' She tried to run, but the strappy sandals she was wearing weren't built for that. Agitated, she started walking fast.

She thought she'd got away. She thought he'd understood her message and maybe headed back to the ship, But when she slowed down she felt a hand on her arm.

'Tasha, please.'

He looked dismayed to see she was crying, and tried to pull her into his arms. 'Hey, I'm sorry.'

'Don't, Quinn! Just...*don't*.'

She pulled her arms free of his grasp and stood there in front of him, feeling like a child, her arms hugging her body. It was like being thirteen all over again. He'd hurt her. The way he'd sat there and told her she wasn't enough. *Again!* He'd *promised*. He'd promised to show her who he really was and perhaps he still really was that bully from all those years ago?

'I should never have said anything. I was… projecting. I was trying to stop you from getting hurt. I…'

She looked up into his face. 'You were projecting *what*?' She felt confused. What did he mean?

You're not her mother.

You need to take a step back.

I was trying to stop you from getting hurt.

'I'm not just another case for you to worry about. I'm not a patient.'

'I know.'

'How close I am to Abeje shouldn't be a concern to you. It should be a cause for *celebration*. That someone out there in this huge, cruel world actually *cares* about her!'

'I know.'

'So why did you say such horrible things to me? I don't understand.'

He was looking at her strangely, as if he were

deciding what to say. If he should say anything at all.

His mouth moved silently, as if he were trying words for size. Trying to build his explanation in his mind first, before speaking the words out loud.

He sucked in a breath. 'I told you about Hannah.'

His wife? What did *she* have to do with this? She remembered him saying their marriage hadn't lasted very long.

'Yes?'

'We didn't get divorced. I know I made it sound like a failed marriage, but Hannah and I were very happy. We married on impulse, but everything was great between us.'

Tasha shifted, looking up at him, wondering what he was going to say next. He'd implied that his marriage was over, but if they hadn't divorced, then that meant…

'She had one or two bad days when she didn't feel great. But she was a strong woman. She believed in soldiering on. It was nothing that concerned either of us to start with. We both worked hard, we were both exhausted, and when she learned that she was pregnant…we put it down to morning sickness.'

He looked at Tasha uncertainly.

Clearly he had never said those words out loud before. This wasn't a well-practised anecdote. This was something intensely private. And painful.

What was he about to tell her?

What did this have to do with her taking a step back from Abeje?

And Hannah had been *pregnant.* They had been about to have a baby.

Tasha could imagine the sort of father Quinn would be—funny, sporty, involved, loving, adoring. She tried to imagine a baby in his arms and her womb actually *ached.*

'You were going to be a dad?'

'Yeah. But she began to suffer terribly—sickness, weight loss, pains, jaundice, exhaustion. We were both doctors, and we both knew that something else was going on.'

Tasha ran the symptom list through her head,

trying to work out what they might indicate. Sickness and exhaustion might have been from the pregnancy, but weight loss? Jaundice? Pain? None of those were good.

'What was it?'

'They diagnosed her with stage four aggressive pancreatic cancer. They did a scan and found metastases in her lungs, liver, spine and brain.'

'Oh, Quinn…'

Stage four cancer meant that it had already spread, as Quinn had said, to other organs. Typically, that would have meant the lungs or the liver, but the aggressive nature of Hannah's cancer had clearly caused a spread to her bones and brain, too. Which she knew meant incurable. Terminal.

'What were the treatment options?'

'They told her that she needed palliative surgery to remove the larger tumours, palliative pain treatment and an immediate chemotherapy. So we would have to abort the baby if we wanted Hannah to have a chance to live.'

Tasha stared in horror. She'd thought his life

had been a breeze. Had imagined that the golden-haired, blue-eyed boy from her youth had just sailed through his life pain-free.

Imagine him being faced with that news. Knowing that even whilst his wife's body was being riddled by a killer disease it had still created the miracle of life.

'What did you do?'

'I told her I'd support her choice. That we could always have another baby, but I couldn't have another *her*. That I wanted her to fight it and to live as long as she could. The idea of losing her…'

He ran his hands through his hair and sank down against the school wall until he was crouched by her feet.

Tasha sat down next to him, empathising with the pain he must have gone through. The joy and the ecstasy of discovering he was going to be a parent and then the crashing diagnosis of his wife's cancer. The knowledge that if they wanted her to live they would have to kill. To go against all they held dear.

'She'd always wanted to be a mum. After being

a doctor that was her dream. And she believed in the Hippocratic Oath so much—about not doing harm—that she couldn't terminate our child. So she chose to defer treatment until after the baby was born.'

Tasha didn't know what to say, so she reached out to lay her hand on his, grasping his fingers and giving them a squeeze. 'Oh, Quinn…'

'I didn't know what to feel. The fact that she was putting off chemo, putting herself at risk, made me angry beyond belief… But then I thought of that baby inside her, who had found a way to live and survive in a body that was under assault from a deadly disease. I wanted our child—of course I did—but I wanted her more. I also knew it was *her* body. *Her* life. And at the end of the day it had to be her decision.'

'It must have been terrible for you both.'

'They operated to remove one of the larger tumours, but when they opened her up they could see it was hopeless. She tried to keep as much of her pain from me as she could…pretended she was okay so she could give our son the best chance at life.'

'It was a boy?'

He nodded. 'But the cancer was too aggressive and she went into multiple organ failure at twenty-one weeks. They kept her going on a life support machine for a few hours, but then her parents and I decided to turn it off. They delivered our little boy, but...' He swallowed. 'He wasn't strong enough to survive.'

Tears were dripping from her eyes, just from trying to imagine his pain and grief. She'd got him *so* wrong. She'd never imagined this pain, this grief, for him. Once again she had spun a fantasy of sunshine and rainbows regarding his life, believing everything had been golden for him.

'I'm so sorry. Truly, I am.'

'I held him in my arms, against my chest. Kangaroo care, they call it. You hear those stories of babies who are dying somehow coming back to life after a parent does that. I hoped for the same. But it was a vain hope. He was tiny. So fragile

I thought he would break! His little hands…his fingers so small! He barely weighed anything. I sat in a chair with him on me and felt his every breath. Including the last one.'

He reached for his wallet and pulled out a photo, passed it to her.

It was well-worn. Obviously it had been held a lot. Looked at a lot. And there she saw Quinn, sitting in a chair, his shirt open, his tiny son—no bigger than his hand—resting against his chest. His son wore a tiny knitted bonnet in a pale blue. Quinn was cradling him. Holding him so gently. His face full of grief and despair.

She'd seen faces like that before. The faces of Maddie's parents. The faces of all those family members she had delivered bad news to.

She watched as tears trickled down his face and then she laid her head against his shoulder, giving him the time he needed.

He had not been afraid to share those emotions with her. She was proud of him for that. For sharing them with her.

She heard him sniff, felt him wipe his face, and then he turned to look at her.

'I've lost someone I love. I've watched my child die. Felt it. It was the most horrific thing in the world. I sat there, concentrating on each breath that he struggled to make, begging him to just take one more. To keep on. To fight through. And it was selfish! *I* wanted him to carry on, because *I* didn't want to face the future without him! I knew that *I'd* be the one to fall to pieces, because watching a child die—it tears you in two. I mean it. It's pain unlike any other.'

She knew. *She knew*! Should she tell him? Should she just get it all out in the open? The way he had opened up to her?

He carried on talking. 'I said those things earlier because...because I've *been* there. I've been the person by the bedside. I've been the one holding the hand of the one I love, watching the last few breaths ebb from exhausted lungs, and you don't want to see that. You *don't*! It's horrible and it takes ages to get past it—weeks, months, *years*! The thought of *you* having to go through that… It almost destroyed me. I left everything to come and work on a hospital ship on the other side of the world because it was the only thing that didn't remind me of home. I'm trying to protect you by saying you need to take a step back. Because—believe me, Tasha—you *don't* want to witness the death of a child. And I don't know if I'm strong enough to help you through it.'

She looked at him now, her face pale, the shadows under her eyes dark. 'You think Abeje's going to die?'

He gave her a look that told her he didn't know. 'Malaria is a killer—I know that. I'm doing everything to save her, but I'm warning you that I might not be able to.'

She laid her head against his broad shoulder again, comforted by the feel of him next to her. 'Thank you for telling me what happened. I know it must have taken a lot for you to tell me.'

'I care about you. Maybe too much. It's muddling my thinking.'

'And I care about *you*.'

She swallowed hard, thinking about what he'd just said. *'I care about you. Maybe too much.'*

Well, if he cared about her then he deserved to hear the whole truth. No matter how painful. She had to tell him. She *had* to! Even if he then saw her for what she truly was. A failed doctor.

'You can't protect me from something that's already happened,' she whispered.

He shifted to look at her better. He was frowning. Not understanding. 'What?'

'I didn't just watch a child die, Quinn.' She looked down at the ground. Away from him. Away from any judgement she might see in her eyes. 'I killed one.'

Quinn blinked. Once. Twice. A third time. Still he couldn't stop looking at her face. Her tear-stained, red-eyed face.

She'd killed a child?

No! That can't be! She has to be wrong!

'What do you mean?'

She gave a shake of her head and then got to her feet, wiping the dust from the back of her skirt.

He got up too, rubbed his eyes and then stood, hands on hips, waiting for her to explain. She *couldn't* have killed a child! She wouldn't be allowed to be a teacher, for a start.

She turned to face him, eyes red.

'I've only been a teacher for a couple of years. I implied that I'd had a variety of jobs after leaving school before doing my teacher training, but that was a lie. I lied to you.'

She'd lied? Only people with something to hide lied.

'But you're telling me the truth now?'

'Yes.'

He believed her. Maybe he shouldn't, but he did.

'I'm listening.'

He couldn't imagine harming someone. He was a *doctor*! He *healed*. He tried to make things better. Taking a life…? He couldn't imagine how that must feel, even though he'd contemplated it to save his wife. But he hadn't had to go through with it. Neither of them had. They had fought for *life*.

'I went to medical school.'

Tasha smiled at him. A sorry smile. A *sorry-I-lied-to-you* smile. Short. Brief. Sad.

'I trained to become a doctor. It was all I'd ever wanted to do after meeting you. After falling in love with you when I was just thirteen and hearing the way you talked about how you were going to change people's lives...'

Her voice almost trickled into a whisper.

'You *did*?'

He couldn't believe it! *A doctor? Tasha?*

'I wanted *my* life to change. Back then I wasn't *living*, Quinn. I was just existing. I had no idea of what to do and no one steering me in any direction. I thought I'd probably end up in some dead-end job, but then Dexter brought you into my world and you talked about all the wonderful things you were going to accomplish as a doctor—delivering babies, saving lives, transplanting hearts, living with a purpose! I wanted that for myself. You made it sound so good. So valuable and important. And I loved you so much I thought you might notice me if I wanted the same things as you.'

He was blown away. 'Tasha, I—'

'It's okay. We were just kids. You never understood how I felt about you. How could you? You'd never experienced my world. You'd never been without love.'

He looked down at the ground, realising just how terrible her life must have been. He hadn't ever thought about it. He'd just been a stupid kid with a stupid ego and he'd almost ruined her life because of it.

'I qualified. I took the oath. I began practising in a large hospital. It was hard. Exhausting. Night after night on call, in an understaffed department, unable to get a toilet break or even to eat sometimes. Some nights I survived on coffee. But I carried on because I knew that what I was doing was noble and worthwhile. And suddenly, for the first time in my life, I felt *important.* Valued. Wanted. *Needed.*'

'You were always important,' he said.

'I didn't know that back then. Like you said, we were kids.'

'What happened?'

He almost didn't want to hear, knowing that as soon as he did her words might make him think less of her. He didn't want to feel that way.

But he knew junior doctors screwed up sometimes. She was right. They were overworked and exhausted sometimes. But they got through it—because if they didn't then people died.

'It was a night shift, and I was the doctor on call. I'd worked two days straight, with barely any sleep, and I'd been beeped to this girl—Maddie—a couple of times already. She had pneumonia, and her SATs kept going really low and she would struggle to breathe, but every time I got to her and gave her some treatment she recovered. Then there was a huge input of casualties into A&E, and I was called to tend to a pregnant woman who was threatening to deliver after abdominal trauma.'

Quinn swallowed, imagining her fear of having to treat that pregnant woman.

'As I rushed to A&E my beeper went off again for Maddie. I stood there in the corridor, staring at it, trying to make a judgement call. The pregnant lady? Or Maddie? Two lives? Or one? I knew Maddie had kept on recovering with the treatment I'd ordered previously, so I called in my instructions for Maddie and chose to go to A&E.'

'I would have made the same choice.'

She gave that smile again. Quick. Brief. A thank-you.

'I was in A&E for a good two hours. The time went so quickly—you know what it's like when you've got to think fast, make immediate decisions, do everything at a running pace?'

He nodded.

'I delivered the baby. It was a boy, and he went up to SCBU until his mum could come out of Theatre. I headed up to Paediatrics to see Maddie as soon as I could, but…'

She faltered, fresh tears dripping down her cheeks.

'Maddie was in respiratory arrest. They'd been paging me but I couldn't answer them. They were frantically trying to get her back. They were doing CPR when I arrived on the ward. I pushed the nurse out of the way to do it myself. I was completely shocked that she'd deteriorated so quickly. Had I missed the signs? Had I misdiagnosed her earlier? Given the wrong treatment? I felt her ribs break. Puncturing lungs that were already damaged and filled with fluid.'

Tasha began to cry with heaving sobs, hiccupping her way through the story.

'I couldn't get her back! I tried! I tried everything. But she just slipped away! She died because of *me*. I had to tell her parents that I'd done my best, but *had* I?'

'Tasha…'

'I walked out of the hospital that night. After I'd told the parents their little girl was dead I walked out. I didn't go back. I couldn't. I knew I couldn't be put in that position again, where I had to make a choice over who lived and who died. Who was *I* to decide such things?'

'It wasn't your fault, Tash. It sounds like you did everything you could.'

'You weren't there! How could you *know*?'

'Because I know you. Because I know what it's like in a hospital when you're on call. I've listened to every word you've just said and I know it's the truth. Because I've seen inside your heart and there's not one shred of darkness there. You did your best. You were put in an impossible position to choose between two lives and I would have done the same as you.'

'But she *died,* Quinn. Because of *me*.'

He took her hands in his and pulled her close, hugged her against his chest. 'No. *Not* because of you.'

She sobbed against his chest. Hot, wet tears soaked into his shirt and he hated it that she was feeling so much pain. All this time he'd been trying to protect her from such devastation but she'd already been through it. And she felt responsible!

He knew that kind of guilt all too well. He'd questioned every decision he'd made after Hannah and his son had died. Especially when Hannah's parents had blamed him for not healing her. For not making a better-informed decision. For not forcing her to have a termination so she could have had the cancer treatment more quickly.

He'd almost been torn apart by guilt, and he'd found himself in a very dark place after the funeral.

Now he understood why Tasha cared so much. Now he understood why she had such a strong attachment to Abeje. It was love. Plain and simple. She had adopted this child in her heart and she was now being faced with losing her if she didn't do the right thing.

'You did everything right,' he murmured, stroking her hair. 'You did everything *right.*'

Soon her crying stopped. Became just gentle sniffs. And they stood there holding one another, leaning on each other for support.

But it was more than just physical strength. It was emotional strength, too.

She needed him.

And I need her.

He'd had to leave her at the school. She had lessons to teach that afternoon and he needed to come back to work, too.

He stood at the end of Abeje's bed, wondering

why she wasn't getting better. Why it was taking so long.

Am I just being impatient? Or am I afraid of the pressure I feel to cure her?

Tasha had completely sideswiped him with her confession. She'd been a doctor. *A doctor!* All this time she'd been on the hospital ship and not said a word. He hated it that she'd kept things from him. Such important things, too. Hiding her pain the way Hannah had. They'd talked about their pasts and he'd hoped that she'd feel she could tell him the truth.

Like I told her everything?

No wonder he hadn't had to explain anything medical to her. All those times she'd sounded knowledgeable, explaining it as internet research. Most friends or family members of patients wanted the doctors to explain the treatments and the medications—what they were, what they did—but she *hadn't.* Because she knew already.

And she was carrying around that guilt born from the death of a child, even though it sounded as if she'd made the right call and done all she could.

But he knew how exhaustion felt when you were just a registrar. Those long hours with barely any sleep or proper nutrition. Soldiering on because you had to…because there was no one else to do it.

How many nights had he stayed up trying to find cures for Hannah? How many medical trials had he hunted down, trying to extend her life?

He'd been there. *All* doctors had been there. And it was awful.

No wonder she was worrying about Abeje so much. She knew what could go wrong! She knew that it was taking a long time to see improvement. When she sat by Abeje's bedside did she see Maddie's face? Was *that* what was scaring her?

But the thing that frightened him most was that he could see a lot of Hannah in Tasha. They were both the same. Both trying to give a child the chance of life more than anything else, even to their own detriment. How many nights had

Tasha sat by Abeje's bed without food or rest for herself?

Rob came over. He looked weary, too, and handed Quinn a chart for him to sign off on some medication.

'The two kids from Mosa are doing well. They managed some real food earlier.'

'That's good,' Quinn said, staring at Abeje and wondering why she wasn't recovering just as quickly.

She was so little. Smaller than the others. Perhaps her immune system wasn't as strong? What if there was something else going on in her system?

'I'd like another round of bloods taken for Abeje, Rob. A full work-up. Everything.'

'Sure thing. I'll get right on it.'

'And I'd like a full scan done. Just to check that there's nothing else going on that's preventing her recovery.'

'Okay, I'll schedule it.'

All children were precious. But the pressure to save Abeje was high. Higher than it had ever been. He would do everything in his power to save her—to stop Tasha having to lose another precious little girl. A girl she saw herself in.

If Tasha felt she couldn't save her, what would it do to her?

Abeje deserved to live. She deserved to fight another day.

He *had* to save her.

He had to save them both.

It felt different boarding the ship that evening. Tasha had laid herself bare to Quinn. She'd told him everything. And that vulnerability felt strange. As if she had nothing left guarding her. Nothing shielding her from harm any more. She was glad she'd told him. That he knew everything.

Outwardly, he hadn't reacted badly.

But had it changed his opinion of her?

He knew who she was and who she had been before. And she'd told him just how much he had influenced her life's choices—how somehow he had always been in her life.

It was almost embarrassing. That a childhood crush had formed her career decisions and she had failed so miserably at it.

Perhaps she'd never been meant to be a doctor? That had been *his* choice, not hers. Perhaps she should have been something else? A sales assistant somewhere. She'd always liked shoes. She could have done something with that.

She'd not been made of stern stuff—hadn't had any of the weapons that doctors needed in their arsenal. She'd never been able to separate herself from the pain and hurt that her patients went through. Had always faltered with the professional distance doctors ought to establish. Had always wanted to comfort grieving relatives. Put an arm around their shoulders. Give them a hug. And then, in solitude, she would cry herself.

She'd been a taut, raw nerve.

Tasha quietly entered the ward, hoping no one would notice her sitting beside Abeje's bed. But Quinn saw her the second she sat down and came over.

She sucked in a steadying breath. No doubt he

would think differently of her now. Perhaps he would consider her a coward. And if that was the case then so be it. He'd never felt much for her before, when they were kids, she could cope with that again. It didn't matter any more. What mattered, she told herself, was this gorgeous little girl in the bed beside her.

'Hey.'

'Quinn.' She smiled.

'How did your afternoon go?'

'It was very nice, thank you.'

'What were you teaching this afternoon?'

'How to write instructions.'

'Oh.' He nodded, as if he recalled a similar lesson himself.

Her gaze drifted over to the two siblings from Mosa, who were both sitting up in bed. 'How are the other children doing?'

'Good. They ate today and kept it down. Always a good sign.'

Yes, it was. But it was just another piece of evidence that said Abeje wasn't eating yet. She wasn't keeping food down. She was being fed through a tube still. She wasn't improving. The worst might still happen.

Tasha shifted in her seat. 'That's great.'

She couldn't meet his eyes. Those beautiful eyes of his that just a short while ago she'd stared into on that mountaintop terrace. How did life change so quickly? So brutally?

'We took some more bloods today. And we did a scan. Hopefully when the results come in they'll give us some good news.'

She nodded. 'Thanks for letting me know.'

'Tash, could I—?'

She held up her hand. 'It's okay. I'm all right.' She retrieved a book from her bag. 'I thought I'd carry on reading to her. It helps, I think.'

He stood there for a moment longer, not sure whether to stay or go. She hoped he wasn't going to ask about earlier. She'd told him the truth, but she wasn't sure she was ready to go into it again. Not this soon. Having Quinn reject her wasn't something she wanted to cope with right now.

He walked away to tend to his other patients and she let out a strained breath. Then she opened the book and began to read, trying to lose herself in a story where nobody died and everyone got their heart's desire.

But she couldn't do it. Her eyes kept leaving the page and looking up to see where Quinn was. For one moment she stopped reading for about three minutes, just staring at him, watching him as he diligently worked on his patients.

You'd have made a great father, Quinn.

Her heart ached for all that he'd been through. What he must have suffered. The picture of him cradling his son had seared itself into her memory. She'd always thought he'd lived such a golden life. He'd had a wonderful childhood home. A family with loving parents. Had known what he wanted to be and done it. Even believing his marriage had ended after only eighteen months hadn't made her think otherwise. She'd believed that he and his wife had obviously been wrong for each other, because he was still here—still smiling.

But there'd been heartache behind his words. Things he'd kept to himself. She couldn't imagine the pain that he and Hannah must have gone through, and then, after losing the love of his life, he'd had to watch his son die just hours later?

She'd thought the loss of Maddie was hard. The fear of losing Abeje was hard. But Quinn had been through real trauma. Real heartbreak. How dared she even *think* that her pain compared?

How did anyone recover from that? How was he still upright?

Why were some people's lives so distressing? When was it their turn to have a little happiness?

She couldn't sleep. It had been a long evening on the hospital ship. She'd read a good four chapters to Abeje before the doors to the ward had burst open and a man had come limping in, with blood running down his leg and a large spike of metal in his thigh.

She'd leapt to her feet, thinking she needed to run over to him, to help him to a bed in order to study the wound and work out how best to remove the spike, but then she had remembered that it wasn't her job any more.

She had sunk back down into her chair as Quinn and his team had leapt into immediate action. Then, knowing that they would be busy, would probably have to go into surgery, she'd slipped away unnoticed.

Now she was at home, sitting with her back against the wall, her knees hunched up to her chest, staring out of her bedroom window as she often did. Trying to decide if anything Quinn had said was the right thing. Whether she ought to take a step back.

She had allowed herself to get close again. She had opened up her heart and that was dangerous. Look at how she was feeling right now. Maybe she should be contemplating leaving Ntembe and going somewhere else? Perhaps it had been wrong of her to let Abeje get inside her heart like this? She never wanted to feel the way she'd felt about Maddie ever again.

Was this what it was like for people who had families? She'd never really had one. She didn't know.

But she couldn't imagine walking away. Not now.

I'm not going to be a coward.

She loved little Abeje. She couldn't leave her behind. What sort of person would *do* such a thing? It would be cruel. And if—*when*—Abeje recovered, Tasha wanted to be there to hug her tightly and let her know that she was loved.

Because she was. And it was important for an individual to know that. They could draw strength from it. They could stop feeling alone.

The moon glowed brightly in the inky sky above, and she could see one or two stars.

Even the moon isn't alone.

Sighing, she slumped down into her bed and pulled a thin sheet over her in an attempt to go to sleep. But the second her head had touched the pillow she heard a knock at her front door.

Who's that?

Her heart thudded loudly in her chest.

She wasn't sure she wanted to open the door in this neighbourhood, this late at night. It could be anyone! She lay there, trying to think about what was best to do. Perhaps if she ignored it the person would go away?

But they didn't. They knocked again. Harder this time.

'Tasha?'

Quinn?

Tasha slipped from her bed and pulled on a thin dressing gown, tying it around her waist. She had a peephole she could look through, and she laid her hands against the door as she pressed her face closer to it.

His hair was ruffled and he looked a little flushed. What was he doing here?

Maybe something's wrong with Abeje!

Tasha undid the lock and yanked the door open. 'What's going on? Why are you here?'

He looked at her, almost as if he was surprised that she'd actually opened the door. But then he took a step towards her, put his hands either side of her face and pulled her towards his lips for a kiss.

CHAPTER SEVEN

OH, MY. WHAT'S HAPPENING? Why is he...? Oh!

She stopped thinking for a moment. Stopped worrying. This moment that she'd first dreamt about at the age of thirteen was actually *happening*! Their kiss outside the maternity wing had been one of comfort. But this… This was one of pure need—desire.

She had always wondered how it would feel.

And now she knew.

It felt wonderful. In his arms. Pressed close.

The feel of him was magical. The feel of him wanting *her.* After all this time. Kissing her, tasting her, breathing her in. It was a heady mix of excitement and elation.

She slipped her hands around his waist and sank into him.

He felt good. Broad and strong. Solid.

It was impossible to think straight.

And then—as quickly as it had begun, as quickly as she had been surprised by the kiss—he ended it, stepping away, looking uncertain. Regretful.

'I'm sorry. I shouldn't have done that.'

Bewildered, stunned, unable to speak because she was still lost in the wonder of that kiss, she simply looked at him, her fingers touching her lips where his had been.

'I had to… You were shutting me out. I didn't like it.'

'I…'

'We were getting close. Becoming good friends. And then you said all that stuff about what had happened to you and suddenly everything changed. *You* changed. It was like you retreated into yourself and took yourself away from me.'

She stared at him. At the way he'd retreated from *her*. He was standing as far away from her as he could, his back against the wall, his hands pressed against it—as if by doing so he would stop himself reaching out to her again.

I want him to kiss me again. This time I'll be ready for it.

'I thought you'd think differently of me. Knowing I'd given up being a doctor,' she said.

He looked confused. 'Why would I do that?' Lines furrowed his brow and then suddenly he looked up at her, realisation dawning. 'Because *he* did—didn't he? Your husband? Simon.'

The pain of that moment from her past flared into being once again. Simon coming home from work the day she'd lost Maddie and asking her why she'd walked out of work… At first he'd been understanding. Knowing what it felt like to lose a patient and how that could affect someone. He had listened as she'd told him how horrifying it had been to take Maddie's parents into that sad little family room and tell them the worst news of their lives.

'We've all been there, Tash. It'll be okay.'

'No, it won't!'

'You just need time—'

'I'm not going back ever again!'

'What?'

'I quit!'

Simon had taken a step back from her, released her, and looked at her with incredulity.

'You can't quit!'

'Watch me.'

And then he'd started staying at work longer than normal. Saying he was working longer shifts. But she'd known what was happening. Eventually a friend had called to let her know what he was up to, and the smell of a perfume that wasn't hers had been a big clue.

'You're having an affair, aren't you?'

'No.'

'Don't lie to me, Simon!'

He'd admitted it. Said he couldn't change who he was—that he needed that release and that she'd changed since their marriage. Had stopped being the fun Tasha he'd always known.

The divorce had gone through quickly—thankfully.

Tasha looked at Quinn, feeling that old hurt—the betrayal, the pain—still in her heart. That feeling she'd carried her whole life.

I'm not good enough. I wasn't good enough for my parents to keep me and my husband discarded me, too.

'That bastard!' The vehemence with which Quinn spoke the word was startling.

Tasha's eyes widened in surprise, and he must have realised that he'd scared her slightly.

'I'm sorry. It's none of my business, of course.'

'It's okay.'

'No. It's not. Look, I'd better go. I just came round to check that you were okay and to…'

His gaze dropped to her mouth and she felt heat rise up within her body as her heart pounded in its cage. Her fingertips were tingling with millions of pins and needles, feeling the desire to reach out and touch him once again. But she didn't. Something was stopping her.

I'm not good enough. He didn't mean to kiss me. It was a mistake. Like everything else. We shouldn't have...

'Quinn?' She said his name as he stepped back outside and began to walk away from her door.

He turned in the street, his eyes twinkling in the dark. 'Yes?'

She didn't want him to go. Didn't want him to leave her. Not again.

She felt her throat and her tongue tighten with all the stuff she couldn't say. Wouldn't allow herself to say. Her feelings for him.

'Goodnight,' she managed.

In the darkness she saw his smile. His shoulders dropped.

'Goodnight, Tasha. I'll see you tomorrow.'

She nodded and watched him walk away. She kept watching until the darkness swallowed him up, then slowly, reluctantly, closed her front door.

The taste of her was still on his lips. What had come over him? He'd gone there because he hadn't been able to stand the awkwardness that had been there between them earlier. He'd felt her pulling away, the same way Hannah had tried to protect him, to make things less painful when the end came.

He couldn't have that happen now—with Tasha.

He needed her. More than he'd realised. He'd gone round to tell her that—to just *say* it, straight out, let her know how he felt, that her past didn't matter—but the second she'd opened her door, looking all ruffled and curious as to why he was at her door in the middle of the night, he'd not been able to stop himself.

He hadn't gone there to kiss her.

He'd been trying desperately to forget the way it had felt to have Tasha in his arms outside the maternity wing.

But tonight…tonight had been startling. Kissing her had been… He shook his head, trying to clear his thoughts, but in doing so he lost his balance. He reached out to grab something to hold him upright, but there was a divot in the path and he went straight over, landing on his left arm.

He heard something break. Felt pain radiate like a burning star in his shoulder and chest. Throbbing. Lightning-bright. Intense. He struggled to his feet, supporting his left arm with his right.

Dammit! I'll need an X-ray.

He'd heard of falling head over heels—but

tripping over a hole in the middle of a street? He ought to have known better. Ought to have brought a torch. This wasn't like England, where there were streetlamps every few metres. The blackness was absolute out here. With just the moon and the stars for illumination.

His shoulder hurt. And his arm, feeling like a giant lead weight, was pulling it down even more.

He trudged on. Imagined how he was going to explain this to the rest of his team.

When he got to the *Serendipity* he'd totally beaten himself up over how stupid he'd been. He should never have gone racing round to Tasha's… he should never have kissed her…he should have waited until he'd got his thoughts and feelings under control before he'd acted impulsively.

But he'd needed to go. Had had to make his feelings clear. It was the only way.

And if he hadn't then he wouldn't be sitting on a plastic chair, looking at an X-ray showing a broken collarbone, of all things.

Maria had smiled at him as she'd put his arm

into a sling. 'I don't know why you don't just tell her you love her.'

He'd frowned. 'What?'

'Tasha! It's perfectly clear to me and to everyone else around here that you two are attracted. It was clear the first day she ran in here, with that poorly little girl. The look on your face!'

'I didn't know who she was back then.'

'No, maybe not. But there was a little something in you that switched on. The light came on behind your eyes. First time I've ever seen it since I've been working with you, Dr Shapiro!'

'It's complicated, Maria.'

'When *isn't* it? Nobody ever said life was easy.'

'We're completely different people. She lives *here*. We'll be leaving in a week or so.'

'You've never heard of long-distance relationships?'

He smiled. 'Yes, but I'm not sure I want to be in one.'

'She could come with us. Volunteer on the boat.'

'She would never leave Abeje.'

Maria sat down opposite him. 'She's close to that little girl, isn't she?'

He nodded, looking across to Abeje, who was restless in her bed.

'Why doesn't she adopt her?'

'I don't know.'

But he *did* know. She was scared to. Tasha was scared of most things. He could see it in her. Scared to commit. Scared to get too involved. Scared to care too much in case it hurt. She thought she could get through this remotely. From a distance. But it was impossible. The world was filled with people, and people made you care.

'I think they'd make a grand pair, those two. If the little tyke pulls through, of course.'

'How has she been since I've been out?'

'Restless. Her fever's building again. We've been trying to keep it down as much as we can, but I think this is her turning point.'

Quinn looked at Maria. Met her gaze.

He felt immense pressure to get this right. The blood results that had come back earlier were good. Abeje's scan was clear. There wasn't anything else going on in her system. She was just a young kid battling a deadly disease. Every patient responded differently.

'Let's see which way she turns, then,' he said.

'What happened to your arm?'

He'd been by Abeje's bed, monitoring her progress as best he could with one hand, balancing her notes on his lap as he wrote with his pen.

Tasha had crept up on him unawares.

Hearing her voice, he instantly stood up, and Abeje's notes, on their clipboard, went clattering to the floor.

Tasha picked them up, scanned what he'd written and looked up at him, frowning.

'She has another fever?' She bent over the girl to rest her hand against the girl's brow.

'We're doing everything we can to make her comfortable.'

'Have you given her acetaminophen?'

'Of course.'

'Has she been seizing?'

'No. She's stable at the moment. Her condition

has neither worsened nor got better over the last few hours.'

'You should have called me.'

'You wouldn't have been able to do anything.'

She shook her head. 'I could have *been* here.' She took a seat beside Abeje and took the little girl's hand. It felt clammy.

'Your arm? You never said how you hurt it.'

'My arm's fine. It's my collarbone that's broken.'

Her face filled with concern. 'How did *that* happen?'

'I tripped in a hole in the road.'

'Last night?'

He nodded.

Tasha could see he was still wearing the same clothes from yesterday. He didn't look as if he'd washed yet, or rested, and she wondered just how on earth he was going to manage any of those things with just one arm.

'I'm not teaching today. I'll stay and help you out.'

'You don't need to.'

'When did you last get any sleep? Have a shower? Eat some proper food? Look, I'm *here*, I've got two hands and, to be honest, if I just sit by Abeje's bed all day I'm going to go mad! Let me look after you for a bit, and we'll both be here if her condition changes.'

The thought of Tasha being around and looking after him was appealing. He *liked* having her around, and he *had* been struggling with his arm in the sling. He'd taken painkillers, but the injury still hurt. The slightest movement seemed to set it off—like a smouldering fire beneath his skin.

And if he was going to feel *any* smouldering heat he'd prefer it to be another kind. Even if that *did* make him feel guilty for thinking about a woman who wasn't Hannah.

'Okay. Thank you.'

'When are you off shift?'

'As of eight hours ago.'

She smiled, understanding immediately. Of course she would. She'd used to be a doctor. You couldn't just switch off when your shift ended. Sometimes you stayed. You carried on to see a patient through. Sometimes you found it hard to let go.

'Right. Let's get you sorted, then.' She stood up, slipping her arm through his good one. 'Show me where your cabin is.'

It was larger than she'd expected. Whenever she'd pictured what the crew's cabins were like she'd imagined tiny rooms, big enough for just a single bed and a sink. Maybe with a small portable television up high on one wall. A small cupboard with a rail to hang clothes. Not much else.

But Quinn's room was a decent size. There was a single bed, neatly made, with a porthole just above it looking out onto the Ntembe docks. Beside it was a small two-seater sofa, a small desk and chair, and opposite a floor-to-ceiling wardrobe for his clothes and a door that led to an en-suite bathroom with a shower and toilet.

He'd made it homely. There was a bed runner in traditional African fabric. A couple of cushions on the couch covered in the same material. And on the desk was a framed photograph of

Quinn and a woman who could only be his wife. Hannah.

She picked it up. 'This is Hannah? She was very beautiful.'

'She was. Inside and out.'

Tasha put the picture down and turned to him. He was standing close and she could feel her body responding to that proximity.

'When did you last eat?'

He shook his head. 'I don't remember.'

'Typical doctor.'

He looked down at the floor, smiling, and her heart just melted. She felt it happen. That simple gesture of his—smiling, looking down—let her see that he knew he was being caught out in how badly he was looking after himself. She felt like liquid. Her body was going to pieces over this man.

'You can't look after patients if you don't look after yourself.'

He continued to smile at her. He had no defence.

'I'll go and get you something to eat from the canteen.'

He nodded, and she sidestepped him and closed the cabin door behind her, letting out a heavy breath, feeling relief flooding through her.

She had to be careful. She couldn't get carried away just because he'd kissed her. He'd told her he hadn't meant to do it. Clearly he regretted what he'd done. But there was something more between them now. She could feel it.

A heat. An intensity. And it was stronger than any silly crush she'd experienced as a teenage girl. This was different. More potent.

More real.

It wasn't a fantasy any more. It wasn't a crush.

She and Quinn had kissed and she could imagine a whole lot more. What she had to do now was keep control of herself, stay logical and remind herself that he would be leaving soon and there was no future for them.

They would both have to keep their hands to themselves.

She found her way to the ship's canteen by following her nose, and returned with a tray filled with scrambled eggs, bacon and toast. She'd also brought two mugs of tea and a small fruit salad.

Holding the tray with one hand, she gave a gentle knock on his door, saying quietly, 'It's me.' And then she went in.

Quinn was lying on the bed, still dressed, his eyes closed. Fast asleep.

She stood and watched him for a moment, gazing at his face, smiling. Feeling a warmth inside her that was making her feel dreamy.

What am I doing? This has no future.

She put down the tray, as quietly as she could and settled on the sofa opposite. There was a book on his desk—some tale of spies and espionage—and she picked it up, intending to read. But once she'd flicked through the first pages—the dedication, the acknowledgements, the first paragraph—she let her gaze return to Quinn. Knowing she could look at him without being caught. Without being judged.

Her feelings for him were growing. Exponentially. But should she be getting involved with another guy? Look how badly it had always worked out for her with men.

It had been such a long time since she'd been in a relationship she was craving it. That closeness. That intimacy. There'd been no one since she'd broken up with Simon. And she'd had a wall of solitude around her for so long that now it was coming down, and she wanted to let him in so badly!

But it was *Quinn*. And her feelings for him had always been muddled since day one. And he'd be leaving soon…

Perhaps I'm just scared? Finding reasons to walk away because I've never been given a reason to stay?

Tasha let out a heavy sigh. She stared at Quinn, taking in every detail of his face, until her eyelids began to droop and she, too, fell fast asleep.

She woke with a start some time later. Quinn was still sleeping and she checked her watch—three hours had passed! *Three!* Okay, so she hadn't got much sleep last night after Quinn had kissed her and then walked away, but she hadn't realised just how tired she was.

Stretching, she got up to work out the kinks in her muscles, and as she stretched her arms high and wide she heard Quinn stir behind her.

'What time is it?'

Blushing, she turned around and sat on the couch. 'Midday. Lunchtime. I brought you breakfast, but you'd fallen asleep by the time I got back.'

'I was beat. But, thanks.'

He tried to pull himself up into a sitting position, but seemed to struggle with just one arm, so she got up to help pull him upright. He pulled the tray towards him and began to eat the cold bacon and eggs.

'I can go and get you something fresh.'

He gave her a thumbs-up sign. 'This is fine.'

She sat down again and watched him eat, but then she felt self-conscious and got up, trying to give him some space. It had been such a long time since she had been close to a man. She couldn't believe she was finding it so difficult to be with him.

When he'd finished eating he swallowed down the cold tea and then began to fiddle with the buttons of his shirt.

'What are you doing?'

'I need to have a wash.'

'Oh.' She watched him struggle for a moment more, but it was painful seeing him fail to undo his buttons with just one hand.

'Here—let me.'

She reached for his last two buttons near his waist, trying not to look at the expanse of chest that had been revealed already. It was making her have palpitations just thinking of what he might look like with no top on.

She went to stand behind him, so she could pull each sleeve off carefully. It was a bit fiddly. She had to release the sling to get the shirt off, but when she did she realised she was staring.

He was beautiful. Not overly muscular, but she could tell he looked after himself. He was trim, with a neat, flat waist, his shoulders were broad and strong, his skin suntanned and golden. When he turned to face her she saw his chest had a smattering of hair in the centre, sun-kissed and barely there.

The urge to trail her fingertips across his skin with a feather-light touch was strong. His nipples were taut and she had to yank her imagination back from the fantasy of wanting to do things to them.

'I shouldn't get this sling wet, so I'll just have a flannel wash. Could you fill me a bowl of water?'

'Sure.'

Colouring, she hurried into the bathroom and smiled broadly at her reflection, shaking her head at all the wicked thoughts that were running rampant through her mind.

I'm a very naughty girl...

She put a bar of soap in the water and let out a big breath before she carried the bowl and a flannel back to him, realising that if anyone was going to wash him down it was going to have to be her.

'I can do my front…but if you could do my back?' he asked, an eyebrow raised.

'Sure.' Did her voice sound as wobbly as it felt?

Tasha watched him wash his chest. He obviously had no idea how erotic it was. Watching him squeeze the flannel with one hand to get all the water out, wiping soap all over his skin, leaving white smears and bubbles that he then smoothed away with the flannel, his skin glistening in the sunlight from the porthole as the fabric brushed over muscle and sinew, his nipples peaking.

He did his chest, his stomach, his face. But he'd need her to do the rest.

She jumped up like a shot.

'Okay. I'll…er…start on your back.'

Her hands were trembling. He couldn't see it, but *she* could. Standing behind him, she looked at his skin, at the line and curve of his spine that she could imagine tracing with her tongue. His broad shoulder blades.

I can't have shaky hands.

She tried to stop it from happening. She ran

the soap over his back, biting her bottom lip, trying not to think of this as a sexual act. Then she used the flannel, feeling the ripple of his muscles under his skin, trying to be tender over his left arm and near his broken collarbone. She wanted it to last for ever.

'I think you're done.'

She didn't want it to be done.

'Shall I get you a towel?'

'No. It's nice to air-dry in this heat.' He looked at her uncertainly. 'I'll…er…do my legs myself. I can reach those. But I'll need a change of clothes. Could you get me something?'

She nodded and turned to open the wardrobe, surprised to see a neat, orderly pile of items, some shirts and trousers on hangers, shoes paired and lined up at the bottom.

'If you wouldn't mind carrying the bowl back into the bathroom for me, I'll finish up in there.'

'Of course.' She smiled, feeling her cheeks blush and thanking whatever god was listening that she hadn't had to soap down his thighs, because if she'd had to do that…

She blew her fringe from her face. Was it hot in there?

In the bathroom, he looked at her uncertainly. 'Er...could you do the button on my...?'

He looked down. At his trousers.

Right. Yes.

She stood in front of him, her hands on the waistband of his trousers, undoing the button, telling herself inwardly over and over, *Don't touch the zip. Don't touch the zip!*

But all she could think of was slowly drawing down the zip and letting her hand slip inside.

When she was done Tasha backed away, closing the door behind her, and sank down into the chair.

What the hell...?

That was probably the most erotic thing she'd done in a long time. How terrible was *that*? That she'd somehow, in all of this, forgotten she was a woman with needs. She'd been so busy shutting everyone out she'd forgotten about who she was under there. Hidden in the dark recesses of her mind. Being alone was all well and good for the majority of the time, but there were other times when she just needed…

She swallowed. Trying not to think of what she needed right now.

She'd been on autopilot for so long now. Cruising through life at thirty miles an hour because it was safe. Becoming a teacher because it was safe. Staying single because it was safe. Shutting down her sexual drive because it was safe.

But now she was in a danger zone. And she didn't know what to do. Or how to react to Quinn. No. She knew *how* she was reacting, but was she going to do anything about that reaction? Was she going to act on it?

From the bathroom she heard a small thump and a small, 'Ow!'

'You okay?'

'Yeah.'

'Well, just holler if you need help.'

He came out wearing fresh trousers, but he held the shirt in his hands. 'Can you help me get this on and buttoned up?'

She nodded, feeling heat surge into her cheeks. 'Sure.'

She stood up and took the shirt, gliding it over his left arm first, so they could get it back into its sling, and then the easier, right arm. Then she stood in front of him to do up the buttons.

Don't look at his face!

The last time they'd stood this close he'd been kissing her. She could feel the heat radiating from his body. He smelled fresh. Manly. A primal scent that she couldn't help but react to as the memory of his perfect chest and body stayed at the forefront of her mind.

'All done.'

'Thanks. I couldn't have done it without you.'

She looked up. Wanted to stare into his eyes for eternity. 'Quinn, I…'

He stared back. 'Yes?'

His voice was thick. Guttural. Had he been affected as much as she? Had he been awakened by the feel of her washing him? Running the flannel over his skin? Having her fingers slip into the waistband of his trousers?

Having her stand *so close*?

His eyes were like pools. She could drown in them happily. She wanted to touch him. To hold him in her arms, if only just for a moment.

But she knew he wouldn't act first. He'd already done that once, when he'd come to her place in the middle of the night and kissed her, and then he'd backed away.

Would kissing him now be a mistake?

Would she be muddling everything they had?

But I want to so much! Perhaps he needs the first move to come from me? Perhaps he feels that by acting first he was taking advantage?

She reached up to touch his face. To run her fingers down his jawline, over his slightly bristled skin. His lips parted and she couldn't help but focus on his mouth. A mouth that had kissed her and could do so again.

She stood up on tiptoe and brought his face down to hers. Unable to fight her doubts for a second longer.

His lips met hers. Delicately. Hesitantly. But then, as if a dam had broken, their lust for one another powered through and Quinn was pushing her back against the wardrobe as her fingers reached for the buttons of his shirt once more—only this time she wouldn't be removing it so gently.

He reached out for the lock on his cabin door.

And she allowed herself to submit to her basest desires.

Back on the ward, they found the parents of the two children from Mosa busy packing up their things. The children sat in their beds, smiling, talking quietly to each other, obviously pleased to be going home.

Tasha stared hard and then turned to look at Quinn, surprised. 'They're going home?'

She couldn't believe this! It was great for them—of course it was—but why hadn't he told her?

The passion they'd just shared was forgotten as she watched the two children get ready to leave while Abeje still lay in her bed, sick.

'Their parents were keen to take them home. They're much better—we think they'll be fine.'

'But...'

Exasperated, she couldn't think of anything to say. Her lips, her body, were still on fire from the intensity of their lovemaking, but the shock of seeing that the siblings from Mosa were about to leave was slowly numbing her once again. It was a clear reminder that whilst she had been cavorting in Quinn's cabin Abeje had still been ill.

I can't believe I did that! What kind of person am I?

She felt hot. Sick. Ashamed of what she'd done.

She went straight over to Abeje's bed, her legs trembling, feeling weak. She would *never* leave Abeje's side again.

It's good that the children are going home. People do recover from malaria.

It didn't always have to destroy and decimate.

She saw Quinn give them a small bag of medication as Maria translated to the parents how and when to give the meds. The parents listened, and before Tasha knew it the staff were waving them all goodbye.

Tasha had no doubt that this family would be absolutely fine. They were lucky. It was all working out for them and they deserved this moment as they walked out through the ward's double doors.

She looked down at the floor, sick with regret. Her moment with Quinn had been everything she had dreamed it would be. He was an amazing lover. The need they'd felt for the other had been overwhelming. But…

His gaze locked with hers and she felt heat rise to her cheeks before she looked away. Abeje had been fighting her fever and yet she had gone to Quinn's cabin to look after him and somehow ended up in his bed!

How could she have done that when Abeje was so poorly? How could she have slept with Quinn when this darling little girl was still fighting and needed her by her side?

I abandoned her…like I abandoned Maddie.

What if something had gone wrong? What if

she had got worse? Deteriorated all alone while she had so selfishly sought comfort from a man. From Abeje's doctor!

I could never have forgiven myself. I already owe the debt of one life. I can't afford to lose another.

Tasha vowed to herself there and then that no matter what happened she would not leave Abeje's side again until she was walking out of this hospital ship to go home.

Quinn had felt elated. For about a minute afterwards. And then the guilt had come tumbling down upon him.

He'd slept with Tasha. The first woman he'd slept with since Hannah. It felt wrong to have done so. And he hated the shame he felt inside.

He'd been the one to get out of bed first, to try and dress himself, but he'd had to stand there whilst she helped him with his buttons again. He'd done his best not to look at her, but when he'd had to he'd tried to smile, hoping she wouldn't see the shame he felt.

When they'd got to the treatment deck and Tasha had seen the Mosa kids were leaving she had bolted for Abeje and he'd been glad for the distance. Glad to involve himself with the kids' departure, ensuring they had everything they needed. When they'd gone he'd turned to look at her, trying to decide what to do, but she'd not been looking at him—for which he was grateful.

I feel I've been unfaithful to my wife.

Logically, he knew that was ridiculous. Hannah was dead. Had been for years. And he was bound to feel this way the first time he was intimate with someone.

Should it have been Tasha?

A woman he'd already hurt?

A woman he felt responsible for?

The woman I...

He couldn't say the last word. Not even to himself. If he said that—if he thought it—it would be like admitting that he might lose another mother and her child.

I don't know if I can do that again.

He'd jumped out the frying pan and straight into the fire.

And sparks were flying.

'Miss Tasha?'

Gasping, she looked up, her eyes locking onto Abeje's in an instant. The little girl's eyes were open and she was trying to smile.

'Abeje!'

She held her tightly, trying not to squeeze her, but feeling such elation that she was awake and talking. She lay Abeje back against the pillow and pressed her fingers to her lips for a kiss, then put those fingers on Abeje's cheek.

'You've had me so worried! How are you feeling?'

'I'm thirsty.' She coughed. 'Can I have some water?'

'Of course! Of course you can!' She turned to Maria, who was standing close by. 'Can you get her some?'

'Of course!'

Tasha turned back to the little girl in the bed.

'Everyone has been missing you so much! You have no idea.'

The corners of her mouth curled upwards, just slightly.

'I've been reading to you. And there's a special book of letters the class wrote. When you've got a bit more strength I'll show it to you.'

'I'd like that.' Abeje blinked slowly. 'I am tired.'

'Of course you are. You've been battling hard.'

She laid her hand against Abeje's forehead. Her fever was down. She'd broken it. Beat it. She was going to be all right. Relief flooded her system in such waves that she thought she might easily be knocked off her feet.

Maria brought over a small jug of water and poured some into a cup. As she did so the ship filled with the sound of an alarm—distant, from another floor.

'Excuse me.'

Maria rushed off the floor. No doubt to an emergency.

Tasha held the cup to Abeje's mouth, supporting her head so that it didn't spill everywhere.

'You're going to be all right.'

CHAPTER EIGHT

ABEJE WAS COUGHING a bit. Sounding chesty. He had to listen in. Just to check. Her lungs were a bit crackly, and he wanted to do something about that.

The pressure to heal Abeje had been weighing heavy on his shoulders. He did not want to feel responsible for ripping Tasha's tender heart in two. He'd not been able to bear imagining Tasha at Abeje's bedside, feeling hopeless as she watched another child die, and to be honest he didn't think he'd have been able to do it either.

He'd feel as if he were to blame. He knew he would. And he couldn't carry the burden of another death on his shoulders.

If he wanted to be with Tasha then she came with Abeje. He knew that. And that was risky for him. He wasn't sure he could allow himself to care for another child like that. So intensely. With his whole heart. She seemed a sweet girl, and Tasha had told him lots about her, but he didn't *know* her.

He wanted to believe that he could. He wanted to believe that maybe he could be happy once again. Be settled, have a family. But…

He watched Tasha as she laughed and smiled and chatted with Abeje. They were so good together. *Belonged* together.

Perhaps it was best if he just walked away?

Sailed away to Madagascar and didn't look back?

Cursing, he draped his stethoscope around his neck and wrote on her chart.

'I'm going to order an X-ray of her chest.'

'You think she's got an infection?'

Tasha's eyes were wide with fresh fear. With the worry of yet another complication in Abeje's recovery. He saw it clearly. Felt it like a punch in his gut.

Heal this child.

'I think she might be developing one.'

'Then we need to get her on antibiotics.'

'We need the films first.'

'But we should start them anyway. What harm would it do?'

He didn't like the way she kept trying to interfere with the treatment. Yes, she might once have been a doctor, but she wasn't one right now, was she?

Dammit, I'm allowing my fear to become anger. At her. For putting me in this position.

'Fine. But I'm still ordering an X-ray. It might take a while. That alarm we just heard will be occupying all available staff.'

It was just him, Tasha and Abeje on this floor at the moment. He'd not been able to attend the emergency call. A doctor had to remain on each ward at all times. He couldn't leave. No matter how much he might want to.

'Do you think it might be pneumonia?'

He didn't want to guess. But it was a good assumption.

'I don't know.'

'Pneumonia's bad.'

'You think I don't *know* that?'

She looked hurt. 'Why are you getting angry at *me*?'

'I'm not! I'm just...' He sighed. 'Let me order the X-ray.'

And he stalked over to his desk to phone the order through. Hopefully the X-ray bay would be clear and they could take her straight down.

Only it wasn't. They had someone in there from another floor. Could he give them thirty minutes?

Sure.

He sat at his desk, staring over at Tasha, wondering what in the world he was going to do.

His shoulder hurt. Quinn took a couple of painkillers and flexed and stretched his fingers. Having his left arm in a sling was a real obstacle. He hadn't realised for how many things you needed both hands. Simple things. Like doing up buttons. Closing the zip on his trousers. Trying to make a cup of tea. Putting on a fresh bandage. Setting up an IV. Trying to take bloods.

He frequently had to get one of the nurses to assist him.

He felt hobbled, and he didn't like it. It reminded him of the time when he was eighteen and had broken his ankle playing football. Being on crutches for weeks had seriously impaired his mood. That feeling of being somehow *less* than he normally was had been incredibly uncomfortable.

He tried to imagine how Abeje felt, lying in her bed, weak and feeble. Not at full strength. He tried to imagine how Tasha must feel, not being a doctor any more.

I'd miss it! Way too much!

He could never stop being a doctor. He could never leave this ship. Well, he didn't think he could. Though he supposed there *were* other medical jobs he could do in Ntembe. Maybe he'd set up his own clinic? That way he could be with Tasha properly and the people here would never be without medical aid. Currently, if *Serendipity* wasn't in dock, they had to walk for days to find it.

But that would be a big step to take.

In fact it would be a giant step! They'd both admitted they had feelings for each other, but he had no idea of the *strength* of her feelings. If he jumped ship to stay behind with her, that would make a pretty big statement, wouldn't it?

'Penny for them?' Rob slumped into a chair next to Quinn.

He looked at his good friend and considered admitting everything. But he wasn't a great talker. If his dad had taught him one thing, it was to button up all emotions. You kept them hidden so you weren't thought of as weak.

'You and Maria…you get on, right?'

Rob grinned. 'Yeah, we do.'

'Working together? Living together on this boat?'

'Yeah.'

'And it's going well?'

'Well, we're engaged, so I'd have to say yes.' Rob smiled and chewed on the end of his pen. 'You and Tasha thinking of making it serious?'

Quinn shook his head. 'I don't know. It's complicated.'

'When *isn't* it?'

'It doesn't look complicated for you guys,' he said.

'Are you kidding me?' Rob leaned in to whisper. 'When I met Maria she was with some other guy. A yahoo paramedic who went base-jumping and bungee-jumping and all that other adrenaline junkie crap. Her family *loved* him. Thought he was a real man. Someone who lived life to the full.'

'What happened?'

'To him? Nothing. He's probably still throwing himself out of aeroplanes. But the thing is she fell in love with *me*, and I worked on this ship, and that meant I was going to be taking her away from her family—which the other guy hadn't done—so they hated my guts. Told her that a *real* man would be a doctor, not a nurse, and that she had to break it off with me.'

'I had no idea.'

'They told her it was me or them. That if she

came away with me they'd have nothing to do with her. Can you imagine that kind of pressure?'

Quinn shook his head.

'She left with me. And though we're happy, and very much in love—as you can tell—she has this constant battle with vicious emails and telephone calls from her family.'

'She sacrificed love for love?'

He nodded. 'Yeah. And I'm thankful for it every day. I know what it took for her to be here with me.'

'Tasha has sacrificed a lot, too.'

Rob leant forward. 'Look. If you want to be with Tasha, then *be* with her. If you love her, if you have feelings for her, if you can't imagine your life without her, then do it.'

Could he imagine life without her now? He thought about sailing off to Madagascar, unable to see her again for a few months. Waving to her from the ship as she remained in port, holding the hand of the little girl she loved so much.

Tasha would bring a ready-made family. She'd come with Abeje—no doubt about that now.

Could he get involved with a mother and child? Put his heart on the line once again?

'She lives *here*.'

'It's gotta be your choice, man. You can save lives anywhere. But your heart stays with one woman.'

'You trying to get rid of me, Rob?' he joked, trying to make the atmosphere less strained.

'No way! You're the kind of guy I'd want in my corner if I ever got sick. But I see how you look at her. How she looks at you when you're not watching. You've got something special. Don't waste it. You have no idea if it'll ever come along again.'

Quinn stared down at the desk. Then he looked up, saw the way Tasha stared at Abeje, with intensity in her searing gaze, desperate for the little girl to get better but fearing a new complication. A new battle to fight for such a small body.

He heard Abeje cough again. It didn't sound good. Alarm bells were sounding in his mind.

Sometimes he found it hard to switch that off—constantly assessing people. Counting respirations. Looking at the sclera of someone's eyes, checking for jaundice.

A million things could give you many clues about a person. A lump low in the throat could be a thyroid problem. A rash could be any number of things from innocent to deadly. Sneezing. Coughing. The sound of someone's breathing. How many breaths they took in a single minute. The way their fingernails looked. The way they walked.

There were always signs a doctor saw, discarded, or became concerned about.

Abeje tried to sit up a bit, so Tasha reached forward to help adjust her pillows. Sitting upright would help her breathing. But she didn't look great.

'Thanks, Rob. I'll…er…have to think about it.'

He wanted to listen in to Abeje's chest again. Maybe start wheeling her down to X-ray. They could wait in the corridor if they weren't ready for them, but it was better to be safe than sorry.

He stepped up to the bed. 'Just whilst you're sitting up, can I have another listen?'

He placed a SATs monitor on Abeje's finger to check her oxygen saturations. It read ninety-four. Which was lower than he'd like. Just to be on the safe side he placed a nasal cannula into her nostrils to give her extra oxygen, tucking the thin tube behind her ears and then tightening the clasp just under her chin before listening in with his stethoscope.

Tasha looked at him, one eyebrow raised, but she sat and took hold of Abeje's hand.

'Now, I don't want you to worry about the work you've missed in class. I'll help you catch up when you're much better.' She smiled. 'I took some photos on my phone of the class. Let me show you what we've been up to.'

Tasha leaned in and turned her phone so Abeje could see.

'This is one of everyone showing their acrostic poems, using the letters of their names. Habib's one was *very* funny! Just wait till you hear it—he's going to grow up to be a comedian!'

Quinn stood beside them, grateful that she was trying to keep Abeje's spirits lifted. He wrote her SATs into her medical notes, but the monitor on her finger was still there and he could see that even with the nasal cannula her SATs were falling.

'Tasha…'

'Look at this one of Claudette. Oh, she was so proud of this painting! Can you tell what it is?'

Tasha hadn't heard the note of warning in his voice. The concern. She was just thrilled to be showing her pictures to Abeje.

The oxygen saturations continued to fall. Ninety-one. Ninety. Eighty-eight.

'Okay, Abeje, I don't think that position is a good one for you to be in. I'm going to give you some full-flow oxygen.' He leant forward to remove the cannula and place the mask over her face.

Tasha sat back as if he'd shocked her with electricity, her face draining of colour. 'What's happening?'

'Her SATs are dropping.'

'What's going on?' There was a note of panic in her voice now.

'I'm not sure.'

He met Tasha's gaze then, and read the question in her eyes. The question she didn't want to speak out loud in case it frightened the little girl.

Is she going into respiratory arrest?

That was *his* fear.

He looked for Rob. He'd been there a moment ago—where had he gone? It was just him and Tasha.

Abeje's eyes closed and her face went slack.

'Oh, my God!' Tasha leapt back, startled, dropping her phone to the deck.

Quinn smacked the emergency button behind the bed and the alarm sounded. He needed to remove the pillows from behind Abeje's head, but he needed both hands—one to remove the pillows and another to steady Abeje's neck. But he was hobbled…one arm strapped to his chest.

'Tasha, remove the pillows. I'll hold her head.'

'Quinn…'

He looked at her. She was terrified. Her worst fears were coming true—so much so that she had frozen, unable to do anything.

But he needed her. Needed her desperately to help him.

'Tasha! Look at me. *Look. At. Me!*'

Her terrified gaze shifted to his face. 'I need you to help me. I need you to do CPR. She's stopped breathing. I need you to help her.'

'I…' Tasha looked down at little Abeje, who lay lifeless and non-responsive on the bed. 'I can't!'

'Yes, you can! I can't do it like this. *Quickly!* Please! If you don't help her now…' He didn't want to finish his sentence. He didn't want to say the words.

Then she'll definitely die.

She was the one who had to do this. He could maybe attempt chest compressions with one hand, but they needed her lying flat. They needed to remove those pillows. Get a backboard so that the chest compressions would have a decent effect.

He grabbed hold of the pillows and yanked. Abeje's head flopped onto the mattress. He couldn't open up her airway with one hand—he needed Tasha!

And suddenly she was there. Her hands crossed over each other, in the centre of Abeje's chest, doing compressions, her face a mask of agony, her tortured voice counting out to thirty as tears streamed down her face.

'I'll get the backboard.'

He ran over to the side of the room, grabbed it off the wall, where it hung in case of emergencies such as this one, and then came running back.

'Help me slide it under.'

He had no idea what had suddenly caused the little girl to go into respiratory distress. It had just happened. But he saw this all the time, and he hated it that he'd known something like this might still happen. She'd taken so long to get better, and she'd always seemed so weak. He'd sensed this. Suspected that something might still go wrong, that she wasn't out of the woods yet.

If she dies...

He couldn't think about that right now. Ifs. Whats. Maybes. All that mattered was following life-saving protocols. Nothing else.

Kids frequently went into respiratory distress.

It was more common for that to happen than a cardiac arrest. But it could *lead* to a cardiac event.

He checked her pulse.

It was absent.

'I'm going to get the crash cart—keep going!'

Tasha was giving her two breaths as he rushed away for the cart, which was on the far side of the ward, and when he returned she was back doing compressions.

'Fifteen…sixteen…seventeen…'

'You're doing great, Tash.'

He reached for the pads, but they were in a pack that needed to be torn open. He couldn't do that with one hand.

'Open these.'

Using the heel of his right hand he continued to do compressions whilst Tasha fumbled with the pack, ripping it open audibly. And he continued to pump up and down as Tasha placed the pads—one near the right shoulder, just under the collarbone, the second just below Abeje's left breast.

Analysing.

The machine paused to read Abeje's heart trace, if any.

Shock required. Stand clear.

Tasha checked to make sure he'd stepped away from the bed, and then she pressed the button with the little red lightning flash on it.

'Shocking!' she yelled.

At the moment the charge was delivered the ward door swung open, smacking the wall behind it, and in ran Rob. He took one look and then ran to them instantly to take over compressions.

Maintain CPR.

Quinn stepped back, exhausted and spent, his injured shoulder raging with pain, but that didn't matter. All that mattered was the little girl.

Analysing.
No shock required.

Rob checked her pulse. 'She's back. I've got a pulse!'

They gave her full-flow oxygen again and Rob

rolled her into the recovery position, constantly monitoring her breathing.

Abeje began to moan as she came to.

Quinn let out a long breath, relief flooding through him as he looked at Tasha. She stood there white as the bedsheet, horror in her eyes, staring at her hands. At what they'd had to do.

'Tasha? You okay?'

She looked at him. A startled rabbit in the head-lights. It was as if she'd just seen something in him that she'd never seen before.

Turning, she bolted from the ward.

He couldn't go after her. He had to stay and help Rob in case Abeje went into arrest again.

She wasn't in the clear yet.

What had just happened?

Tasha couldn't believe it. One minute they'd been smiling and looking at pictures, and the next…

It had turned into a nightmare.

A nightmare!

Her worst fears…

She'd been depending upon Quinn to keep Abeje safe. Trusting him with her, trusting the medication, trusting in his care, and it had been hard for her. The worst thing she'd ever had to do because…

Because she'd tried to save Maddie and she had failed. But she had tried to save Abeje and she had started breathing again. They'd got her back.

Her belief in her own abilities was changing, and she'd realised something as she'd pumped up and down on Abeje's chest. Something that had become quite clear as she'd tried to save the little girl's life.

She *needed* Abeje to survive—not just because it would be awful if she died, but also because she was beginning to believe she could have a family. Beginning to believe that she could love again. Beginning to believe that she was worth caring for.

And she couldn't lose her family.

Not just Abeje, but Quinn too.

She'd been through some tough times in the

last few years, but she was still here. Still upright. Still trying to live and love.

She already loved Abeje, but she wanted to love Quinn, too.

He'd helped her to get Abeje back. They'd done it together. And she'd seen in his face, in his eyes, in the depth of his soul that he was trying everything he could, trying his utmost to bring Abeje back to her. One of her most precious loves.

It wasn't shock at the realisation that Abeje had survived—it was shock at the realisation that she'd put herself out there again…for him. To give him her heart…to give him her trust, her love.

Only he didn't want it, did he?

She'd seen the regret in his eyes after they'd made love. The guilt he'd felt. The shame? She had almost felt him backpedalling away from what they'd done when he'd got out of bed and asked her to help him put his shirt back on. He'd barely been able to look at her.

But the life or death crisis over Abeje had cleared the veil from her eyes. Her heart beat for *him*. It always had. It was probably in sync with his, both beating like hearts in a mirror.

And he was discarding her once again. Discarding her as her parents had. As Simon had. As he had when they were teenagers. Only back then she hadn't slept with him. Now she had, and that hurt even more.

Abeje's crisis had made her see her own.

She couldn't look at him.

Couldn't bear the idea of meeting his gaze.

That was why she'd run away, needing fresh air, needing space to get some perspective on what she would have to do.

Abeje will want me by her bedside.

But still she couldn't go in.

I don't need to see the goodbye in his eyes.

She'd cared.

Loved.

Had given her heart to him.

And now it hurt. Hurt as if someone had reached inside her chest, ripped her still-beating heart from it and then crushed it right before her eyes.

A low, keening groan escaped her lips as she bent double, almost unable to breathe.

This was it.

This was what the pain felt like when you lost everything.

She couldn't go back.

She couldn't face anyone.

Not Abeje, not Rob, Maria.

Not Quinn.

None of them.

Because she was a failure. Everyone else had always known it but her, it seemed.

She couldn't do this.

She didn't have the strength.

Now Quinn would see her for what she really was.

A coward.

And he would leave her—just like everyone else in her life had already done.

Quinn wiped the clammy sweat from his brow and sat down, exhausted. His shoulder burned like nothing he had ever experienced before. A white-hot ball of fire. But it was nothing to the pain of the emptiness he felt inside.

Tasha had scared him. The way she'd stood there frightened, frozen in fear, when he'd needed her to help him. Needed her to help save Abeje! He'd not been able to do it alone, he'd needed her help. When she had just stood there like a statue for one terrible moment he'd thought he'd have to try and do it alone, and if he'd had to do that, with just one arm, try to do CPR and apply pads and provide breaths, he knew he would have failed.

Abeje would have died. His worst fear would have been realised.

Thankfully Tasha had leapt into action—but that pause, that hesitation, that inability to move had terrified him. He'd not been ready to lose that little girl and he'd certainly not been ready to give in. *He couldn't have.*

Because he'd known if he had to wrap his arms around Tasha one more time to stop himself seeing her heart torn asunder he would be lost.

He'd be hers.

Totally and utterly.

And that scared the hell out of him.

He'd loved a woman and a child before. He'd made them his everything. And when he'd lost everything he had known how absolutely soul-destroying it could be. There was no way he wanted to go through *that* again.

But they'd been lucky. They'd worked as a team, they'd saved her life, and then Rob had arrived to provide relief and there had been more hands, and Abeje had been breathing again, and…

She was stable for now. They'd done a scan and discovered that Abeje had fluid in her lungs—he wasn't sure if it was a result of the parasitical infection or not at this moment, but they were treating her now. She was awake, her face covered by a high-flow oxygen mask, and she was talking. Sore, but talking.

Quinn was sure that she would be okay. It had been tricky there for a while, but he believed her crisis was over.

And Tasha was nowhere to be seen.

Abeje was asking for her. Missing her. They'd grown close, those two, like mother and daughter, and Abeje wanted her 'mum'—like all kids when they're sick. Tasha was the closest thing to a mum that Abeje would ever have.

Well, if she couldn't have her mum…

He slipped into the chair at the side of Abeje's bed and took her hand in his, cradling it as if it was a jewel. Stroking it. Trying to convey with the power of touch his concern, his love.

'Miss Tasha's just getting some fresh air. You know you scared us?'

Abeje nodded. 'I was scared, too.'

'I bet.' His heart bled for her. She was so strong—so brave! So…

And that was when he realised. He didn't just care for Abeje because she was part of Tasha's package—he cared for Abeje because he really *cared* about her! He didn't want her to be hurt. He didn't want her to feel frightened and alone and now he had stepped in. Stepped over the mark that doctors should not cross and taken up the mantle of a *father*.

It shocked him.

Scared him.

But, although the shock of adrenaline that hit

his system made his legs feel weak, he also re-alised something else about himself.

It's okay. I can do this.

He *wanted* to do it! Wanted to expose himself in that way to the terrifying reality of being a parent again—but he wanted to do it with Tasha. She was his beating heart. His soul. His life. He couldn't live without her. Even now, with her gone, it was unbearable!

Sure, he'd felt guilty after they'd made love—but wasn't that to be expected? It had been his first time with a woman since his wife.

He didn't want to leave either of them.

He needed to let Tasha know how he truly felt.

'I'm going to get Tasha. Bring her back to the boat,' he told Rob as he came to Abeje's bedside to adjust her drip.

'All right, mate.'

It was like an oven outside as he strode out of the cool air-conditioned ship and into the heat of the African sun. His painkillers were just start-ing to take the edge off his pain, but they weren't touching the pain he felt in his heart at the thought that he might not get her to come back.

He expected to have to go all the way to her house, but as he stomped down the gangplank he saw her at the bottom, sitting on the bonnet of his rusty car.

She looked up. Saw him coming and then madly wiped her eyes and got up to walk away. 'Please go away. I don't want to see you.'

'We need to talk.'

She spun round, glaring at him, her eyes watering. 'How's Abeje?'

'Stable. Asking for you.'

'I can't go in looking like this. Tell her I'll be in soon.'

'You look amazing.'

'*Don't!* Just…don't. None of your pity, please. I know how you feel and you don't have to tell me twice. I'm used to rejection, and I'm particularly used to rejection from *you*!'

'I love you, Tasha Kincaid.'

It felt good to say it. To say it out loud. And proud. He didn't have to hide from those feelings any more.

'*What?*' she looked at him, incredulous, through blurred red eyes.

'I love you. From the top of your curls all the way to your toes. I love you and I want to be with you.'

She blinked. Confused. Shook her head. 'But after we…'

'I was frightened. I felt guilty about Hannah. I hadn't been with anyone since she passed away. You were my first. I was shocked by how it made me feel. But what we just did—we saved a life! Saved *Abeje's* life! It's made me see just what I don't want to lose. I've always tried to avoid this. Mothers and their children. And for the most part I've been successful. But you, Tasha, you came into my life like an explosion of feelings I wasn't ready for. You confused me. Made me second-guess myself. I wasn't sure what I was doing half the time. But then we saved Abeje, and, I held her hand, and I realised that I was ready. Ready to love again. Ready to be a partner. A husband. A father. I can do it. But only if I have you by my side.'

She wrapped her arms around her waist. 'People I love always leave me.'

He stepped up to her, unpeeled her arms and took her hands in his. 'Not me. *Not me.*'

She looked at him uncertainly. 'You mean this? It isn't a joke? One last joke on Nit-Nat? Because if it is then you're being very cruel.'

He kissed her hands. 'I mean it.'

'What if I'm not good enough? What if you realise that after all this time I really am just Nit-Nat? The girl you despised.'

'I never despised you. *Never.* There was nothing wrong with you, Tash. That was all *me*, being stupid. Like I've been stupid these last few days, allowing fear and shame to control me as it did all those years ago. But you make me strong. If I have you then we can get through anything together, and I just know—if we let it—we could have a great future.'

'But you're leaving soon.'

'No. I'm not. I'll stay here. What if…? What if we build a clinic together? So the people we love here can have medical care when they need it—not after a two-day walk in forty-degree heat, or after waiting for a ship to pull into port? We can build our dreams *here*, Tash. Together. What do you say?'

She seemed to be thinking about it. Keeping him in agony until a small smile began to build upon her face.

'Tell me you love me again.'

He let out a breath and beamed her his best smile.

'I love you, Tasha Kincaid. Now, tell me you feel the same.'

'You always were the root of my problems, Quinn Shapiro.'

'But…?'

A smile broke across her face. 'But I love you.'

He scooped her up and whirled her round, then put her down only to cradle her face and kiss her.

'Right. We can celebrate later. Right now there's a young girl that wants to see you.'

He took her hand and began to pull her up the gangplank.

'Quinn?'

'Yes?'

'Thank you. For everything.'

He smiled.

EPILOGUE

'WE DON'T WANT to be late. Have you got your shoes on?'

Tasha popped her head into Abeje's bedroom and saw her daughter fastening the buckles on her sandals.

She held out her hand. 'Come on.'

Wearing sunhats and their finest dresses, they left the house hand in hand.

'Will Daddy be at the clinic?'

'Yes. He had to get there early. He wanted to do one last check on the place before we open it up to the public.'

'And I get to cut the ribbon?'

She smiled. 'You get to cut the ribbon.'

Abeje was so excited about being the one to open the clinic. But it seemed right. They'd thought about getting the town leader to do it, but they wanted someone close to them to do it. They'd adopted Ntembe as their home, and Abeje as their daughter, so it seemed only right. It wasn't favouritism, or nepotism. This was her home. Her city. She'd lived here before they had.

The long dark days of malaria were behind them. Abeje had grown big and tall, thriving in the warmth of a loving family. The day the adoption papers had gone through had been the happiest of their lives. Their next dream? To open this clinic!

A crowd had gathered outside, and it took them some time to work their way through it to the front. There were so many people Tasha knew now, and they all wanted to stop her, say hello, shake her hand or kiss her on the cheek. Thank her for what they were doing for their community.

Tasha was incredibly excited, nerves tumbling around in her stomach. She couldn't wait to see Quinn. Couldn't wait to stand by his side.

And then she saw him, dressed in a white shirt and khaki trousers, ensuring that the yellow ribbon stretched across the entrance was fixed securely for the grand opening.

'Quinn!' she called, beaming when he turned round and smiled at both of them.

He held out his arms and Abeje went running into them. He scooped her up, hoisting her onto his hip.

'You're getting a bit big for this now.'

'Never!' Abeje laughed.

'Well, when my back gives out we'll stop, okay?'

'Okay.'

He kissed her on the cheek and then put her down, reaching out to embrace Tasha.

She sank into his arms happily.

Today was a great day.

They'd had many great days together. The day Abeje had left the hospital…waving goodbye to the *Serendipity* as it sailed out of port, leaving Quinn by her side…moving in together…getting married…adopting Abeje.

And now this day. The opening of their clinic. Their dream.

It meant so much, what they would be able to do—not only for this community but those around it. Cutting down treatment times, getting healthcare to those who desperately needed it. And they'd even got a small team of trucks to use as mobile hospitals, after remembering the trips they'd taken out to Mosa and the more remote villages.

Many lives were about to change for the better.

As were theirs.

Tasha kissed Quinn, revelling, as she always did, in holding him close, feeling the strength of his love for her.

The intensity of their love for each other was overwhelmingly wonderful. She'd never felt anything like it. She had a family of her own. Was this what other people had? This happiness? This *belonging*?

'I'd better make a start, then.' Quinn said.

'Good luck.'

She let go of his hand as he stepped up onto a small podium and the assembled crowd grew quiet. A sea of expectant happy faces looked up at him.

Tasha handed Abeje the pair of scissors she was to use for the ceremony. 'Stay with me. Wait for Daddy to finish.'

'Hello, everyone! Welcome to the Ntembe Clinic! It's good to see so many of you here today. So many familiar faces.'

Tasha could see Maria and Rob in the front row. They stood holding hands, beaming smiles up at their old colleagues. It was good to see them here. They'd taken leave from the *Serendipity*—just for a month for their honeymoon—and they'd promised to be here, despite no doubt having many more important things to be getting on with!

'My wife Tasha and I have long held a dream to open up a clinic here. To serve you—our friends, our family, all the people we have come to know and love here. We hope it will become a vital site—not just for healing, but for education and support for everyone.'

They certainly had grand plans. They wanted to teach here. Teach communities about safe sex, about immunisation, about first aid practices and how to do CPR. They wanted to run a volunteer centre here, a blood clinic, a midwifery centre, and most of all they wanted to accept medical students—to give them the education and experience they would need to advance in the medical world. It wasn't just going to be a clinic to patch people up and send them on their way.

'So, without further ado, I would like to invite my daughter, Abeje, to do the honours and open up the Ntembe Clinic!'

He stepped down from the dais and moved back so that everyone would be able to see her cut the ribbon.

Shyly Abeje stepped forward, and held the ribbon. She looked up at her father and he nodded encouragingly. Then she took the scissors with both hands and with a huge smile cut through it. The two pieces fluttered to each side as everyone behind her cheered and clapped their approval.

'Well done, sweetpea!' Tasha took her hand and together they stepped into the clinic. Their brand-new, clean-as-a-whistle clinic, with the crowd following in behind them.

She felt a hand slip into hers. Quinn.

'This is it. The start of everything.'

She smiled, looking back at him. 'It is.'

'Was my speech too short, do you think?'

'It was perfect. It's too hot to stand out there listening when everyone wants to be inside to see it for themselves.'

'You're right. As ever.' He kissed her cheek.

They stood there, accepting congratulations from everyone who passed. They shook countless hands, thanked hundreds of people, it seemed, and spent hours explaining what each room was for, what services they'd offer, and said that everyone was welcome—whether they could afford to pay or not.

And when the crowds were gone, and the last person had said goodbye, the three of them stood in what would be the waiting room of the clinic and looked about them.

'Can you believe we did it?' asked Quinn.

'Yes,' she said. 'Because we did it together.'

He stroked her cheek. 'I couldn't have done it without you, Dr Shapiro.'

'Well, in a few months you might have to,' she answered, her cheeks flushing as her hand went to her belly and she began to tell him the secret she had held inside her since discovering the good news just a few short days ago.

He frowned. Then his eyes widened. 'You're pregnant?'

She nodded. 'About ten weeks.'

He pulled her into his arms and hugged her tight.

She was so happy that he was thrilled. She'd been dying to tell him, but had thought that telling him today would be the best thing. She'd wanted to be sure. And it had taken a few days for it to sink in with her, too.

Her own baby. Her own flesh and blood. She'd never had that.

Tasha kissed him, looking into his eyes, and then she knelt down, beaming at Abeje.

'You're going to be a big sister!'

* * * * *